ashley erin

why
not me?

books by ashley erin

All or Nothing series
All About Us
All About Hope

Rule series
The No Asshole Rule
The No Bad Boy Rule
The No Jock Rule

Standalones
without walls
The Fine Line Between Love and Hate
Why Not Me?

dedication

To Jessi
Thank you for taking this journey with me.
No one knows how much I put into this book, except you.
You were there for the tears.
For the times I wanted to delete it.
For the many, many, many rewrites.
For the emotional breakdown.
And, finally, for the moment I finally reached the point I could say this is my best book yet.
I love you.

prologue

Circling my hips, I spin in a circle as Dawn and I dance together. We're out celebrating Dawn's new job and the fact I aced my marketing exam. Lifting my arms above my head, I give a little shimmy, jumping when I feel my phone vibrate in the back pocket of my jeans.

Without missing a beat, I pull it out and smile when I see the name on the screen of my cell, I swipe my finger with an eagerness that hasn't dissipated in the nine months we've been seeing each other. We fell hard and we fell fast, but I've never felt so connected with someone.

"Hey, babe, one sec," I yell over the pounding dance music. It's so loud, I don't know if he can hear me, my words probably faint under the vibrating bass. Dawn smiles as I turn, waving at Blake when she glances at me,

I hold my phone up and point to the patio. She grins with a wink and goes back to dancing with a giant of a man.

The patio is lit with twinkle lights, random heaters sit next to the picnic tables filling the space providing ambient heat for the rare person brave enough to face the bitter cold. The music sounds through a few speakers along the wall, but it's turned down to be background noise. Tucking my free hand under my arm, I stand under the heater next to the door.

"Sorry about that. Is everything okay?" It's unusual for Landon to call when he knows I'm out with my girlfriends. That must mean things didn't go well with Melissa. "Do you need me to come over, we can cuddle on the couch. I know tonight wasn't easy for you."

Snowflakes start to fall around me, the first snow of the year making today one of my favorite days. I love the snow. There's something enchanting about the first snow. It blankets everything to create a crisp, clean canvas. The air is fresher, and it's the sign that mother nature is preparing for new growth. I think the only season I love more than winter is summer, when everything is in full bloom. The reward for the months we've endured the cold.

The music shifts to something slow. It's quieter outside, the soft melody over the speaker adding to the magic of the night. I feel free of more than just another exam under my belt. Knowing that we can finally move forward, it makes me tilt my face up into the crisp flakes and smile. Tonight, everything is perfect.

When nothing but silence comes from the other end of the line, I can barely hear his breathing, I check my phone to make sure we didn't disconnect. "Landon? What's going on? You're worrying me."

"I can't see you anymore, Allie." His words are cold and detached, almost as though he's talking to a stranger, so different from this morning.

I can't stop the sharp inhalation at his words, the frigid air burning my lungs as I stumble to the nearest picnic table. No one is outside, the cold October night making everyone shy away from spending too much time outdoors—something I'm grateful for as my eyes fill with tears.

"What are you talking about? This morning everything was fine. What about everything you've told me, said to me?" My voice cracks as I try to make sense of what's going on. Why is his tone so disconnected? My voice lowers, filled with such confusion and pain that I can't recognize it. "I'm so confused."

"There's nothing to understand. I'm sorry I let this go on as long as I did, it was a mistake. I guess hindsight is twenty-twenty." A whooshing in my ears blocks out his voice, the tears I've been holding at bay begin to fall as I realize this isn't some weird, cruel joke. It's real.

"I see. I guess there's nothing to say then." My voice is faint, barely a whisper, my head already filling in the blanks. I knew this was a risk, I was stupid enough to think our connection was strong enough to withstand *her*. So much so, that I did something I never thought I would do. Ever.

Wrapping my arms around myself, I bite back tears of despair. This is what I get for pushing aside my initial reservations and falling for his pretty words.

"Goodbye, Allie—I'm sorry." The last words are whispered, a slight crack in the cold façade, but the phone clicks silent and that slight crack means nothing as I'm left sitting on the cold wooden bench in shock.

I slump against the rough edge of the tabletop, it's sharp corner digging into my spine as I stare mindlessly as the snow slowly builds up on the ground, its beauty now tainted with the quiet breaking of my heart.

chapter
one

Seven Years Later

Shutting down my computer, I feed my fish, Bernie, and click all the lights off in my office. Before I set the alarm, I shoot Brendan a quick text letting him know I'm on my way home. He insists, especially in the winter.

> **Brendan:** Please drive safe, traffic is insane today. Despite its return every year, people seem to forget how to drive in the snow.

It doesn't matter how much time passes, Brendan never wavers in his interest in my safety or how my day is going. Smiling despite the weight of exhaustion settling into my muscles, I send him a heart emoji and tuck my phone away in my purse.

Taking a quick glance around, I lock up before walking sluggishly to my car, my feet dragging in the flats I was wise enough to toss under my desk. It's been a long and exhausting week. We had to fire another developer for the new park this week, setting us back three months of work. A setback we didn't need when we were already behind schedule.

The drive home passes by in a blur, my windshield wipers clearing the falling snow, but visibility is still terrible. It's really coming down, again. One more thing to ruin my week, I hate the snow and the foot that's fallen over the past three days just sours my mood even more.

Parking in my spot, I wait until the song on the radio is over before shutting my car off. The silence is welcome, my phone was ringing off the hook at work and the second I walk in the door I know Brendan will want to hear about my day, which I love, but this is my time to clear my head, especially after a day like today.

I love my job, but when I need to go over termination papers with a guy I genuinely like it's not enjoyable. Then, to top it off, I had to field calls from the companies who donated to the park fund and explain why we're behind schedule and over budget.

Sighing, I adjust my scarf and hat, before sliding out of my car. The pavement is icy, and the fluffy snow gets in my shoes as I slide around to the front of my car to plug it in before making my way to the passenger side and grabbing the straps of my messenger bag and purse from the back seat. My car beeps twice as it locks, the lights flashing brightly in the night.

Despite the cold, I find myself frozen on the spot as the snow falls around me. I'm normally a happy go-lucky person, but on this day every year I'm full of melancholy. It doesn't matter that it's been seven years, October twenty-fifth is always full of memories and confusion. The sting of the hole still in my heart never disappearing, no matter how full and good my life is.

My brain doesn't let me turn off the replay of that day. From the morning full of smiles and giggles, to the night when my heart was broken. To top it off, I'm then filled with guilt because I have an incredible man in my life, a man who should make me forget Landon.

Tilting my head back, I look to the brightly lit windows of the condo I share with Brendan. Our building looks sketchy from the outside, the battered front door is grimy and the stucco covering the walls is crumbling away.

I remember when Bren and I first stood outside the front door, staring up at the building and debating whether we even wanted to go inside. I have that feeling now, but this time it's because I don't want Brendan to feel the sadness I'm carrying. It's not fair to him that after all this time, a part of my heart is still broken.

Taking a deep breath, I make my way into the building and focus on the memory of the first time Brendan and I walked through these doors. The entryway is plain, just simple linoleum and a set of mailboxes for all the condos. The hallways are all painted the same builder's beige, simple, nothing fancy, but a lot cleaner looking than you would expect after seeing the outside.

As I reach the door to our condo and step into the spacious living room, I remember the smirk on the realtor's face when she saw our jaws drop. There is no way we could have been prepared for what awaited us inside.

The inside is in complete contrast to the outside. Sleek, modern, bright, and incredibly spacious. All the units were newly renovated when we purchased it.

I step inside looking around the room and remembering it when it was empty. It was beautiful when we bought it but comparing the empty space of my memory to the warm home we've created over the years, I love it even more than the day we moved in.

The gas fireplace is on in the living room, its radiant heat welcome after the frigid cold outside. Soft music comes from the kitchen, along with the mouthwatering scent of garlic and spices.

Hanging my bags onto the coat rack just inside the door, I unwind my scarf and remove my jacket. Hands reach out, offering me a glass of merlot, before resting on my shoulders and massaging them gently.

"You look tired." Brendan's voice is warm, the soft timbre comforting.

Turning, I tilt my chin up to receive the kiss I know is waiting for me. Brendan smiles down at me, love and affection radiating from him as he runs his hands up and down my arms to warm me up. I feel a little of the wear of the day fall away at his touch. Somehow, he's always been able to piece me together, just enough that I don't completely crack.

"It's been an exhausting week. We fired Martin today, which added a stack of official paperwork to my already towering pile. Three months and we haven't even broken ground on the new park, now we're delayed until spring which means I've been putting fires out with our investors." Closing my eyes, I groan at the fresh reminder of how many people yelled at me today.

Bren tsks appropriately, his fingers winding with mine as he leads me into the kitchen. Sitting in the chair he pulls out for me, I watch him move around the room. It's been this way since we moved in two years ago. He's home before I am and loves to cook, so whenever I walk in the door he hands me a glass of wine, asks me about my day, and puts the finishing touches on whatever delicious dish that's waiting for me.

"How was your day?" I sip my wine, savoring the rich

burst of flavor.

"Good. I'm on my way to getting this couple approved for a huge mortgage, which means an incredible commission. I was thinking, it's been a long time since we've gone on vacation. Maybe we can finally take that trip to Italy you've always talked about." He smiles at me, voice full of pride.

"That would be nice, there are some amazing places to see." I try to infuse a little more enthusiasm into my voice as I continue to watch him move around our spacious kitchen.

I'm searching, always searching. The internal battle begins as it has for over a year now. I love him. I do. It's just lately we haven't felt like us, something is missing and I can't pinpoint what exactly it is. And on this night especially, I really feel it, because if something wasn't missing, I wouldn't be so sad over what was.

The thing is, he loves me so much and I don't want to hurt him with these doubts, especially when I don't know the answers. I think I'm just tired, maybe we do need a vacation and Italy would be so amazing, especially if we could take our time and really see everything we want. It's been several years since we've gone away, not even camping, and I think getting away and spending some real quality time together, exploring and having fun, will help alleviate these doubts.

Sighing, I run the tips of my fingers over the stem of my glass, wishing for the hundredth time that this day didn't still bring so much sadness. Gazing outside, I focus on the way the lights reflect on the windows of the patio doors, blocking out the view of the park on the other side of the parking lot. Blocking the view of anything except the safety and comfort of this home. The safety and comfort of Brendan.

"Are you okay? You're in your own little world." His soft, comforting voice breaks into my thoughts and I realize he's been talking to me.

Guilt fills me. He deserves so much more than I'm giving him right now, than I've been giving him in longer than is acceptable. "I'm sorry, this whole ordeal has been wearing on me. Paul is interviewing new contractors next week and I'm supposed to be meeting with possible sponsors for the new recreational facility rather than meeting with contractors to outline the park." The lie slips out easily, because that's what I've been thinking about in between thoughts of Landon—cringing, even his name hurts to think—and that night. Sipping my wine, I stand to help him set the table. "Tell me more about your day."

He fills me in on the rest of his day, beaming as he tells me about signing the final paperwork on another couple's mortgage. It's their first home and the pride he feels in helping them achieve that dream makes his eyes shine. He has a huge heart and he always strives to help everyone who contacts him in any way he can. It's how he approaches everything in life and it's one of the things I love most about him.

Brendan sets steaming dishes onto the table. The sight of roasted asparagus, mushroom risotto, and chicken seasoned to perfection makes my stomach growl. I worked through lunch today, only eating half of my sandwich before my phone ringing off the hook stole my attention.

"This looks incredible, as always." I smile at him, appreciating how he seems to just know when I need the comfort of my favorite dishes.

We eat silently, the scraping of the cutlery on our plates the only sound in the apartment. Brendan finishes, kissing the top of my head before disappearing into his office. It's our routine. Friday nights he works, so I clean the kitchen and then find something on television to relax to.

Tonight, though, I wish we weren't so predictable. How

did we get to the point where we can share an entire meal and not say a word to each other? How does that happen?

Scooping some coffee into the machine, I finish wiping the counters and the stove while it percolates. Adding a splash of milk and the smallest amount of sugar, I take it into his office.

Running my fingers through the mess of curls, I brush his hair away from his forehead and set the coffee beside him. I watch him work a bit, playing with the soft strands of hair, wanting things to be different and not sure what to do. "Can that wait until tomorrow? Maybe we could watch a movie."

Surprise flits across his face, replaced by an ecstatic smile. That look destroys me. After six years together, it's easy to take him and what we have for granted. We're at a level of comfort that easily becomes complacency and I don't want us to become so complacent that every day is mundane.

"I would love that." He sounds so eager, I promise myself to try a little harder and not take him for granted. Brendan starts closing programs. "Why don't you go pick something to watch? Your choice."

Turning, I head into the living room and load up a comedy while he finishes shutting down his computer. Tucking my legs up onto the couch, I wrap a blanket around myself and get cozy. Brendan sits on his side of the couch, looking longingly at the empty space beside me. Pushing play, I shift over and curl into him. I'm not typically into cuddling, but I feel the need for his warm comfort and, based on the look he's giving me, he needs it too.

Brendan brushes my hair aside, kissing me on the cheek before holding me closer as the movie starts. We watch, wrapped in each other's arms until the toll of the day finally takes me down.

Stirring as I'm lifted, I blink sleepily up at Brendan as he carries me to our room. Glancing at the clock on my nightstand, I'm surprised to see it's after midnight. He sets me on my feet and I sleepily change into sweats and a tank top. I can feel Brendan's eyes rove over me appreciatively as he strips down to his boxers.

Crawling into bed, I curl up on my side facing away from him. The bed dips as he lays down, his body heat warming my back when he inches closer. Lips trail kisses over my bare shoulders and rather than the tingling of excitement, I resist the urge to pull away.

"Bren, I'm exhausted and I'm meeting Blake and Dawn at the market early tomorrow morning." A resigned sigh brushes across my skin as he moves away, lying on his back.

Closing my eyes with a sad sigh, I reach over and grab his hand. Squeezing it gently in apology, I regulate my breathing until I finally start to doze off.

It should be Brendan's face I see behind my eyelids, but it's Landon's piercing gaze that taunts me well into sleep.

* * *

"Allie, come and look at this! You should totally buy this for Monique." Blake waves me over from the booth I'm browsing in. Several people around us look at her with amusement. She's the more boisterous of my two best friends, comfortable being the center of attention. In fact, she revels at being in the spotlight. She should've been an actress.

Every week the convention center fills with booths. Various vendors renting the space to show their wares. Hundreds of tables with artwork, homemade soaps, fresh baked bread, cupcakes, and anything else you can imagine.

Crossing the aisle, I grin as I see the object in Blake's

hand. It's a small wooden jewelry box with Celtic designs intricately carved over its surface. My sister is obsessed with everything Celtic. "This is a perfect Christmas gift. I was at a loss of what to get her this year."

Taking the box, I carry it to the vendor and pay what seems like a small amount for something so beautiful. Slipping my hand through the handle of the paper bag that is handed to me, I loop it around my wrist securely as I follow Blake over to the next booth to join Dawn.

Dawn is bent over some homemade cupcakes, her eyes glazed over as she takes in the various flavors.

"What happened to cutting back on the baked goods?" My voice is teasing. We all know Dawn will never give up cupcakes, They're her kryptonite.

Dawn and Blake are identical twins, but they couldn't be more different. Blake is outgoing, a physical education teacher who also teaches drama. Dawn is more reserved. She's quiet and enjoys listening more than talking, which is why it's surprising that she's one of the top real estate agents in the city. I think it's because she has amazing intuition, she can read between the lines of what people say to her and get to the root of what they want or need in a home.

"Shut up. I need them if I'm going to survive our mother's visit." Laughing, I wander away when I see brightly colored scarves and beanies a few booths down.

Running my fingers over the soft wool of a seafoam green and purple scarf, I debate whether I need it. Screw it, taking it off the rack, I also grab the matching beanie and wait to pay for my purchase.

Adding the bag to my wrist, I turn to join my friends as we work our way through the aisles, weaving through the crowd of people making their way down the same path we are. By the time we leave, our arms are full and all my Christmas shopping is done. I also feel much better than

I did yesterday. They gave me the distraction I needed from the turmoil I've been facing and as I listened to them gripe about numerous dating disasters, it helped me remember just how lucky I am to have someone as wonderful as Brendan.

Hugging my friends goodbye, I wrap my arms around myself, scowling at the snow as I hike to my car. The morning with them was perfect, relaxing, and filled with laughs. Yet the sight of the white blanket shimmering in the sun still manages to sour my good mood. The parking lot is treacherous, black ice covered in a layer of fluffy snow. It's so deceptive in its appearance. I slide a few times before I finally make it safely to my car.

After it warms up for a few minutes, I ease my way out of the stall and through the parking lot. I've just turned onto the side street, my car slipping a little as it tries to find its grip when a blaring horn sounds behind me moments before my car is jolted forward. My head slams into my steering wheel, dazing me.

Frantic knocking breaks through my haze, muffled words through the glass as the handle to my door shakes.

"Hey! Are you okay?" More knocking, before I hear a low, "Shit."

Leaning back in my seat, I groan as pain shoots through my temples and down my neck. Fumbling with the handle, I swing my legs out the door and breathe in the fresh air before I look up at the person before me.

My throat seizes as I meet familiar blue eyes staring down at me in concern, a wave of dizziness causes me sway on my feet. Dizziness I'm positive has nothing to do with hitting my head.

The expression of shock on his face is probably the same look I'm wearing as I lose the ability to speak. It feels like my lungs are collapsing, every breath a painful struggle. I haven't seen this face in seven years. Okay, that's a lie. It's a face that haunts me, one that I have barely been able to push aside. And even when I successfully make it a day or two without thinking of him, my dreams fill in for my mind.

Every time I think I've finally started to forget, a song will come on the radio or a face with just enough similarities will jar my memory and send me spinning. Landon Taylor has haunted me and my pieced together heart for the better part of a decade.

My lungs burn as I gasp in the frigid air. The familiar burning behind my eyes that's always present when I think or dream about him. The same burn that turns into tears on the very rare occasion I succumb to curiosity and look him up on social media.

"Allie . . ." That voice, its deep resonance sending shivers down my spine as my heart begins to race. Even though it's been so long since I've heard his voice, my body reacts intensely to the way he says my name. The scent of his cologne, the same cologne from my memories, assaults me. A sweet, woody fragrance, with just a hint of citrus.

I say nothing, my body is numb except for the ache in my chest as I stare at him. He left a hole that's never quite been filled, no matter how much time passes. His eyes search mine as I drown in the memories I've forced myself not to think about.

Lips press against mine feverishly as he lowers me to the ground, our bodies grinding together in desperation. Voices carry through the trees, reminding me that this is a stolen moment, a risk we're both taking.

"Oh God, I've missed you." His voice is thick with need.

The damp grass is cool against my back, but the rest of my body is flushed with heat. I don't care that there are people who will notice he hasn't come back to the bonfire with me, I only care to satisfy this need to be close to him.

Our tongues dance together, he tastes of rum and coke, and I'm addicted. My fingers grip the long strands of his hair, pulling him into me, desperate, needy.

His lips slow against mine before he regretfully pulls away as his friends start calling his name. "I love you, Allie."

"Allie. Allie!" Landon's concerned voice breaks through the pain of the memory and I'm once again lost in his blue eyes. My voice seems to have completely disappeared.

"Allie, you need to tell me you're okay. Is there anyone I can call?" His gaze is concerned as I stare at him blankly, fine creases forming between his brows when I still don't say anything.

Shaking my head, I drop my eyes to my hands to release the hold his gaze has on me.

"I'm okay. And no, I don't want to call anyone." The words are choked out, full of pain but not from the impact of his car rear-ending mine.

I should call Brendan, but I need to get my shit together first.

Brendan.

It was four months after Landon tore out my heart that he managed to break his way in. We shared a university class and became fast friends, his sweet, genuine demeanor so likeable. I knew he liked me, but I wasn't in a position to open my heart again.

By the end of the semester, I knew he was in love with me. I didn't return the feelings, but my soul fed off the way he made me feel—loved and safe. A year later and he asked me out. We've been together ever since. His steadfast personality, his genuine and kind soul eventually won my heart. A comfort I crave right now.

Closing my eyes, I ground myself before standing and pressing my back into my car cringing when I look back up at him. My body is tense, my head throbbing. I can't differentiate between the physical and emotional pain I'm experiencing right now.

"Crap, I knew I hit you hard." Landon's fingers brush over my forehead where I'm sure a ghastly bruise is forming before he lowers them to gently press into my neck.

Every muscle stiffens as he probes, the pressure of his fingers sending tingles down my spine. My body remembers exactly what those fingers are capable of. "Please stop, I'm okay," I whisper, not bothering to try and hide my anguish.

"No, you're not." He drops his hand, the frustration in his voice making it rough. "Look, it's cold and I have an appointment to make. Here's my information and here's my business card. You're going to come and see me tomorrow for an assessment at ten in the morning. If you don't show up, I'll come to you."

He shoves a business card and piece of paper into my hand, wrapping his fingers around mine until they're closed.

My hand tingles as he takes his away, turning and walking back to his car. I watch him the entire way, my eyes devouring the sight as every inch of me hurts more the further he moves away. He looks back at me when he reaches his door, his eyes never leaving mine as he gets into his car and sits there, waiting.

Swallowing hard, I drop back into my seat, shut my car door, and drive away without even examining the exterior damage. My predictable life has managed to change directions so abruptly that I feel like everything is about to be overturned.

chapter
two

Landon

Watching Allie drive away was more painful than when I broke my leg three years ago, and almost as painful as telling her we couldn't be together. She's been a constant in my mind since the last morning I saw her.

Allie's skin is silky under my fingertips as I rub her back. She moans, pressing back. I increase the pressure, her low groans turning me on. Hell, everything she does turns me on.

"I'm going to end it with Melissa, tonight when you're out with Blake and Dawn." Pressing my lips between her shoulder blades, I talk into her skin.

She turns in my arms, the smile on her face brilliant. "Really?"

Kissing her, I hold her close. "Yes. I love you. I don't want to be with anyone else. It's something I should've done a long time ago, I'm sorry. I know you haven't felt good about all of this."

Her face fills with guilt. "I feel like such a horrible person. I hate being the 'other woman.'"

I hate the fact that I've made her the "other woman." She's shown a lot of patience while I try to figure out how to end things with Melissa, but truth be told I haven't been ready and I should've told Allie I wasn't, but then she would've moved on and I just couldn't handle that thought either. If I am really honest with myself, I've been a selfish ass.

"Tonight, I'll fix all of this. I promise." She smiles when she hears how sure I sound. It's time I make this right.

That night I not only broke my promise, but I also broke both of our hearts.

Seeing her today, everything about us just came flooding back. She still makes my heart speed up, her soft voice is a caress on my strained nerves. The flush that fills her cheeks when we look at each other is still there, and the craving to talk to her and hold her and laugh with her, it's a physical need.

Whenever I try to banish thoughts of Allie away to dissect later, my mind fails me. She might not even be the same woman I remember, time changes people, yet the feeling I had the first time I saw her is the exact same one I had when I saw her today.

Like my soul recognized its missing piece.

Tomorrow I'll be able to spend some real time with her, maybe I can finally give her the apology she deserves and not a pathetic one given over the phone after coldly ending things.

I can't stop hope from filling my head, maybe I'll finally get the second chance I've craved all these years. I know from stalking her social media there was a boyfriend at one point, but her profile picture has been the same for over a year now, one of her standing next to a waterfall, so maybe he's out of the picture.

When I get home, I log in and search for Allie's social media profiles. I can't help it. I wish her profile wasn't as secure as it is, even though I know it's smart.

Josh leans over my shoulder and groans, "You've got to be kidding me."

"Shut up. I rear-ended her today, she's coming in tomorrow so I can check out the damage. Seeing her brought back a lot of memories, and now I have my chance to make things right, to fix my mistake." I click on her profile picture and scroll through them.

"Do you see that guy? He's in years' worth of photos. Do you honestly think that nine months with you outweighs years with that guy? Don't you see how messed up this is? Refer her to someone else. Let her live her life." Josh points at the photo I've stopped on. Allie is sitting on some guy's shoulders, her hands tangled in his curly hair. They're both in swimsuits and smiling at the camera. The date on the photo is from four years ago.

"Josh, I can't. I just—I need to be near her." My voice comes out strained, desperate. He doesn't get it, he doesn't understand the connection we share, the one I threw away. Now that I have my chance to see her, I won't give it up. We've never been able to resist each other and this need isn't going anywhere.

"You're an asshole," he growls.

"I know, but that's not going to stop me from seeing her. Even if it's just one more time." I sigh.

This is my chance. I'm not going to throw it away.

chapter three

Allie

Waking up after an awful night's sleep, I drag myself out of bed toward the bathroom. Glancing behind me to a sleeping Brendan, his curly hair sticking out all over the place makes me smile. The hole in my heart that was reopened yesterday afternoon has a Band-Aid over it. The safe comfort of Brendan's arms preventing me from leaping into a black hole of memories.

The same arms that put me back together, protecting the cracks from breaking even further all those years ago, held me together once again last night. It kept that question that taunted me for years, *why not me,* from resurfacing.

Brushing my teeth, I avoid looking in the mirror. I'm mad at myself. I'm angry that I'm so weak a person that someone from my past still has so much power over my emotions. That he still holds a large piece of my heart, even after he stomped on it. That even now, I'm still wondering *why not me,* even though I shouldn't be.

After seven years, I should be able to look at him and be angry that he ended things over the phone, or better yet, not feel anything at all.

I should be able to look at the man who has loved me for six years and realize I have what I need. Yet, I can't shut off the way he still permeates my thoughts on a regular basis. I've tried. I've tried every single day since that night.

Yanking a brush through my hair, I relish in the pain I deserve as it rips through the tangles.

He chose someone else. Someone he said I didn't need to worry about. He picked her, not me. Brendan picked me. He loves me, every part of me. With him, I'll never need to wonder or doubt his feelings. He is safe, he loves me, he makes me laugh, and we have a wonderful life together.

"Good morning." Brendan walks into the bathroom, stretching his arms above his head before wrapping them around me. Looking up, I'm surprised to see he looks sad. His voice is muffled as he speaks into my hair. "You didn't sleep well last night."

Closing my eyes, I breathe in his comforting scent. "I had a nasty headache from the accident. I'm going to see a physical therapist this morning."

Angling my head when he leans down to kiss my neck, I smile into the mirror as our eyes meet and ignore the wrenching guilt about not telling him the full story behind the accident.

"Do you want me to come with you?" He turns me to face him, lifting me onto the counter so he can step between my legs.

Panic fills me at the idea of Brendan seeing me near Landon. He knows me too well, he'll know something's up. Clasping his shoulders, I lean forward to kiss his cheek. "Nah, enjoy your morning. I don't know how long I'll be."

He smiles as he kisses me once more before turning to switch on the shower, the warm steam doing nothing for the chills running through my body.

I finish getting ready for the day, tying my hair into a messy bun before throwing on sweats and a hoodie. It's tempting to dress up, but I won't give in. I shouldn't need to impress him.

Maybe there's a silver lining to this weird and uncomfortable situation. This will give me an opportunity to finally have closure on the Landon issue. That's what I've needed all these years. A chance for the door that was left slightly ajar in my mind to finally shut. Not that I would ask him why he picked her instead of me, but an opening to say a real goodbye, not a heartless sever over the phone.

Two hours later I'm parked outside of Landon's clinic, Freedom Physical Therapy, trying to find the strength I need to go in, get evaluated by Landon, and get out unscathed and hopefully ready to finally let go.

Slinging my purse over my shoulder, I take a few calming breaths before leaving my car and entering the building. No one is at the front desk, in fact the entire open space is empty. This is my opportunity to leave, to walk out and not look back. I start to turn, but before I can take a step Landon comes out of an office I didn't notice in my cursory glance.

"Allie, I'm glad you made it." His eyes scan over me, a trail of heat following the path of his gaze. He steps in close, pressing his thumb into the tender skin around the large bruise on my forehead. Before I can think about what I'm doing, I'm leaning into his touch, my eyes drifting shut.

There is something unique about the way his hand feels on my skin. The connection is powerful, the draw instant, and I find myself falling into another memory.

Landon is kissing my neck, specifically the spot that instantly makes me moan in need. The palms of his hands rub my back, before pressing into my lower back to pull me into his arms. It's a stolen moment, one we shouldn't be taking, but all common sense and morality flies out the window when we're together.

"Allie . . ." His words are tortured. He needs this as much as I do, but his guilt is starting to eat at him. He needs to make a choice.

With a sharp breath, I jump back as I think about the consequences of what's happening. He probably hasn't thought about me since that night, or if he has they've been fleeting thoughts that don't matter. He let go of us. Unlike me, I've never quite let go. Tears fill my eyes as pain shoots through my neck, but the pain in my heart is even worse.

"Oh—shit—ow." The words are a low groan, the pain in them a mixture of physical and emotional.

"I hit you pretty hard yesterday. Hang your coat over there and then sit on that exam table over there." The gravelly tone of his voice reminds me of every time we were together. It's the first indication that he might be as impacted by my presence as I am his.

I hang my coat, the burn of his eyes as they track me feels familiar. When I turn around, I let myself meet his gaze straight on. He's intent, his blue eyes darkening as we stare at each other. I examine every feature, every twitch. And I see it. He feels everything I feel.

The realization that this feeling isn't one-sided is overwhelming. For so long I told myself I imagined our connection, but I know I'm not imagining this. So, what changed? What happened that night to make him so cold? Why her when the connection we have is so intense, so consuming?

Landon is leaning against the door of his car when I leave work, chewing on my lower lip, I lock up with a barely restrained smile. He grins when he sees me, his long legs closing the distance between us. Waving goodbye to my coworker, I wrap myself in his arms.

"I didn't think I was going to see you today." Closing my eyes, I breathe in the yummy scent of his cologne.

"I told Melissa I was going to wash my car. I needed to see you," he rasps, the desperation we feel in these stolen moments evident in his voice.

Pain lances through me at the mention of her name. I know the situation is complicated, but I wish we didn't have to sneak around while he deals with the end of their relationship.

He feels me stiffen in his arms.

"This isn't forever, Allie. I promise. We have something here, something that's been missing in my life. I just need more time."

He always needs more time, but when he tilts my head back and brushes his lips across mine, I let it slide. I know they've been through a lot together, I just hate this place we're stuck in. It was never meant to go so far.

"Okay," I agree. It feels wrong, but the idea of losing him is too painful. Maybe this time he'll follow through.

He locks the door, the loud click distracting me from the memory. My stomach fills with knots as I walk over to the exam table. Licking my lips, I hop onto the smooth, vinyl surface. Unable to tear my eyes away from Landon, I watch every movement he makes as he picks up a clipboard and pen before striding over to me.

His fingers start probing my neck, pausing when they get to my thundering pulse. I'm looking over his shoulder, avoiding the bright blue gaze I know is trained on me. He sighs, continuing his examination as he asks the question I was both hoping he would ask and wishing he wouldn't.

"Should we address the elephant in the room?" His voice is cautious, quiet.

He continues his inspection, his eyes on what he's doing while I ponder what I really want. I can feel him look at me as minutes pass and I still don't say anything. When he comes to stand in front of me, I finally meet those brilliant blue eyes and I can't look away. I always loved his eyes. They're the color of sapphires, but the iris is rimmed in a gorgeous green. There's heat there as they flick between mine, and the urge to lean forward is like a force pushing on my back.

"It's been seven years—are you sure you want to rehash everything?" Now that the offer is on the table, I don't know if I can handle what he has to say, even though I know I need to hear it and he needs to say it. Face to face. The truth, out loud.

"I wasn't talking about that, I was talking about how, after all this time, our attraction hasn't lessened and how badly I can tell our lips want—no need—to touch right now." His hand wraps around the back of my neck squeezing in the way that makes me dizzy with want, his head tilting down as my pulse takes off again.

Heat flares in my belly from a low burn to an inferno.

For a brief second, I find myself leaning in, my chin lifting out of instinct, but then I freeze. I'm a horrible person. With tears in my eyes, I turn my head at the last moment. The soft press of those full lips against my cheek breathing a fire into my soul I haven't felt in so long.

"Landon, I can't do this. I have a boyfriend. I can't—I won't go through this again." I choke out the words, my voice cracking. "The last time shattered me."

He breathes in a shaky breath as he drops his hand, his

eyes somber. "Our timing has always been shit."

Nodding, I grimace at the motion. "Maybe we should just finish up here."

Silence falls as he completes a variety of movement tests. The only words are requests to move my body this way or that way. By the time we wrap up, I have a list of exercises to complete three times a day and a demand to return in a week.

The door beckons, an escape from this torture. Slipping my feet into my shoes, I pause when Landon speaks from behind me.

"Allie, every moment from that night, every moment since I hung up that phone after hearing your voice for the last time, I've been filled with regret. I'd like to explain myself, if you'll give me the chance." He lifts my jacket from the rack, holding it for me while I slip my arms into the sleeves.

A shiver runs through me when he runs his hands down my arms, almost as though he can't help himself, or maybe it's completely unconscious, the same way we used to just move together. This is how it's always been between us, this spark that neither of us seem capable of denying. It's intense and explosive, and it's wreaking havoc on my heart.

I look up at him, hugging my arms around myself. "Okay." The word is barely audible, but Landon hands me his cell phone, primed for my phone number.

Typing it in with shaky hands, I give it back to him and slip out the door with a quiet "goodbye."

It's just for us to get closure. It means nothing.

chapter four

Landon

A small, bouncing ball of gray fuzz greets me as I walk in the front door. Crouching down, I pick up PeeWee and hug him to my chest. "Hey, buddy!"

He snorts as he licks my cheek before wiggling to get down. I rescued PeeWee four years ago when he was five. No one wanted him because he's a mutt with only three legs. Grinning as he brings me a toy to throw, I pick it up and toss it down the hall. Not even a missing leg slows him down as he scrambles after it.

Tossing my jacket onto its hook, I go into the kitchen to grab a beer before dropping onto the couch. My cell finds its way into my hand, Allie's contact information filling the screen, before I realize I was looking for it.

Seeing her again just reminded me of what I already knew, I should've never let her go. I made a choice, I should've stuck with it, but I was young and foolish.

Memories of that night have haunted me since I hit "end" on the call.

Melissa is crying on the couch, her eyes following me as I hold my cell up to my ear and walk out onto the balcony.

The dial tone rings for a while before Allie's voice comes on the line, muffled by loud dance music.

Shit, it's girls' night out and here I am taking the cowards way out. I know if I tried to do this face to face, I would never be able to follow through, but I need to. My life—it's just not simple anymore.

The music is cut off, her soft voice coming across the line. I can hear her smile in how her voice sounds, but I couldn't tell you what she's saying. Turning to look into my apartment, I see Melissa typing away on her cell. Her face is flushed from her tears.

Clearing my throat, I try to detach myself from the situation. "I can't see you anymore, Allie."

Her voice changes, hurt filling it as she expresses her confusion. I say what I need to say to cut myself off from her before hanging up. Dropping my head into my hands, I allow myself a moment to grieve. This is not how this evening was supposed to go.

The door slides open.

"Is it over?" Melissa asks.

Nodding, I force myself to turn around.

She steps toward me, wrapping her arms around me. It feels wrong.

"Let's just forget this happened, move on. We need to." My arms hang limply at my side, I can't bring myself to return her embrace.

"I know." My voice is rough, but I take the hand she offers and follow her into the apartment. She's right, in order for this to work we need to have a clean slate.

"You're home. How did your self-torture go?" Josh appears in front of the blank screen of the television, a mocking smirk pointed in my direction.

Clicking my phone off, I lean my head back onto the cushion of the couch. "Shut up. It's the least I can do after rear-ending her. Besides, she's with that guy still. Anyway, I'm going to see her to explain what happened and we can leave it at that."

"Whatever, bro, I may be younger than you, but it's clear that I have the higher IQ. You've never been able to let her go, not really. And if she's involved with someone, you being in her life is a mistake. Just let her go." He crosses his arms, giving me a pointed look.

"Mind your own business," I snap. "We're not the same people. We're older, wiser. I like to think we won't make the same mistakes."

His words hit me where it hurts, because I know he's right. The chemistry between us is off the charts. I don't want her to do anything she'll regret. We've already made the mistake once. My words feel hollow even to my own ears, seven years later and nothing has changed, at least in how she makes me feel.

Downing the rest of my beer, I get up and head to the basement. Wrapping my wrists, I beat my frustration out on the punching bag. Somehow Allie and I have avoided running into each other for seven years, but less than a year after Melissa and I break up for good, suddenly our worlds have collided again.

Why does she have to be with someone? I don't want to lose her from my life again. Telling her we were over was one of the worst moments I've experienced, and the only reason I was able to do it is because I took the coward's way out and did it over the phone.

Typing in my code, my phone lights up to Allie's information and I open a new message window.

The letters of the keyboard taunt me as I debate what to write. Shaking my head, I laugh at myself. It feels like I'm nineteen again.

Me: When can we have that discussion? I'd like to clear the air, maybe be friends?

Friends. That word sucks, but I won't let her go again, so if friends are all we can be, then friends will have to do. There's something about Allie, she fills a void I don't know I have until she's taken it away.

Allie: Friends, huh? We tried that seven years ago. We snuck around, nearly destroyed a relationship, and several people got hurt. That's how great of friends we made.

Me: I was nineteen, you were twenty. I think we're more in check with our hormones now.

Allie: I'm with Brendan right now, and I snuck into the bathroom to text you. It feels like foreshadowing of what's to come. Or maybe a flashback of what was.

Me: It doesn't need to be like last time. Think about it and get back to me. I miss you. We were friends first, Allie.

Allie: Look, I want to know what happened. I think closure is a good idea. As far as friendship, let's see how our chat goes. If we decide to be friends, I'm going to be open with Brendan about it. Friends or not, he needs to know and feel comfortable with it.

Me: When can we meet?

Allie: Tomorrow. Brendan is meeting with some new clients, so I'm free.

When I rejoin Josh in the living room our older

brother, Kellan, is sitting with him on the large leather couch. He looks up at me from the laptop situated on his lap, his eyes narrowed into thin slits. "You're a dumbass."

"Hello to you too, big brother." I drop down onto my spot and pick up the remote, scrolling through our library of digital movies, ignoring my brothers as they stare at me.

"Josh told me what you're doing with Allie. There's no way this ends well, for either of you." His critical tone grinds on my already shot nerves. When he shuts the computer and sets it onto the table, I know he's not done.

"You don't know what we're talking about. I'm going to explain to her what happened, and then we're going to be friends." Crossing my legs at the ankles, I finally decide a re-watch of *Community* is in order.

"A single man and a taken woman can't just be friends. Not with the past you two have. You're not nineteen anymore, the mistakes you make are no longer cute." Kellan arches his brow at me.

Ignoring him, I hunker down to watch one of the best shows ever while trying not to count down the hours until I can finally have a chance to explain myself to Allie. An opportunity I never thought I would get.

He chuckles to himself, trying to get a rise out of me. It nearly works, but I bite my tongue. I'm not about to take advice from a dude who is twenty-nine and has never been in love.

Allie's the one who got away, and I'll take her any way I can get, as pathetic as that sounds.

* * *

Helping PeeWee out of my car, I set him on the ground and make my way to the entrance of the park where we arranged to meet. I'm early and Allie is nowhere in sight, so I sit on the bench, lifting PeeWee into my arms when he scratches at my leg.

I'm talking to him, rubbing his chin when I hear her voice behind me. "I'm pretty sure bringing the world's cutest dog is illegal when you're meeting your ex-girlfriend to explain why you broke up with her over the phone." Her tone is sarcastic, but lightened by the smile on her face as she comes around the bench to face me.

She sits next to me and reaches out to pet PeeWee. He leans into it, his brown eyes closing as she finds the spot on his neck that he loves to have scratched.

Allie looks stunning in a black down coat, red scarf, and matching beanie. Her dark brown hair falls in waves over her shoulders, my hands itch to reach over and feel the silky strands. I loop PeeWee's leash around my wrist for something to do with my hands, otherwise my fingers would be running through the waves.

"He needed his walk." I shrug, unashamed that I brought him to soften her a bit. I knew her defenses would be up and this little scruff muffin has a knack for making even the most hard-assed people smile.

"Well, let's walk." She stands up, tucking her hands into her pockets.

We fall into stride next to each other, silent as we enter the trail. The cover of the trees shelters us from the frigid winter wind. Our breath fills the air with white fog as we walk.

"Remember when we met and started hanging out how I was seeing Melissa? And then when we realized our connection and we became more, you knew I was still involved with her?" At first, there was a bit of a thrill to seeing two different women, until I realized the connection I had with Allie was real. Then it became obvious I needed to end things with Melissa.

That was harder than I anticipated, given our history. We met in high school, hung out in the same crowd, and

I helped her escape from her house when her parents were going through a brutal divorce. And then once I came to terms with the fact that it was no reason to cling to the relationship, there was always something going on in her life that made me feel guilty about leaving. She had surgery. Her grandma died. I could never find an opportune moment.

"Of course, any morality flew out the window. When I was with you, I couldn't think of anything other than how you made me feel. Besides, I believed you when you said you were waiting for the right time to break it off with her." Her brows pinch together. "Then you finally told me you were going to do it, but you chose her over me in the end. Why her, Landon? Why not me?"

I hate the sadness in her voice, the hurt that still lingers after all this time.

"After you left my house that morning, Melissa showed up at my door a few hours later. I'd invited her over because I was planning on ending it with her, like I told you I was. Before I could, she handed me a pregnancy test. It was positive." My stomach clenches as I remember seeing her that afternoon, looking absolutely devastated.

She confronted me over Allie, calling me out for cheating on her and threatening to withhold access to our child. She wanted me to commit to her, give things a chance, and even though I knew things with her would never be quite what I had with Allie, I also knew that we had been happy before.

Allie inhales a sharp breath, her eyes shooting to mine before returning to the path. Her breaths start coming faster, and I'm not even sure she's aware that she's walking faster, her face closed off.

Without giving her too long to think about it, I push forward. "Melissa told me she knew about us and wanted me to choose her, and our child. She thought for the baby's sake we should try and felt that what you and I had was something that would pass. Allie, I was nineteen and I knew how hard it would be for her to raise the child on her own. How hard a single parent has to work, even if the other parent is involved. It took me all day to prepare myself to let you go. And even then, I was a coward and did it over the phone. I knew if I saw you, I would never follow through." I don't try to clear the thickness from my voice. The memory of that day haunts me. So many mistakes were made. Mistakes that paved the way for nearly a decade of my life.

This time Allie spins to face me, her cheeks rosy and her eyes glassy. "You have a kid? I knew you hadn't broken things off with Melissa, but I didn't think—" She cuts herself off as she shakes her head, a tear spilling down onto her cheek. "I was so foolish."

"I'm sorry. There's so much I would change if I could go back, I know it's a lot to ask for you to trust that, but it's the truth." I hate the look of betrayal she's directing at me.

There were so many secrets, so many lies. And I'm not even done with the shitshow that happened after Allie was out of my life.

"That's what I believed. I moved Melissa into my apartment, prepared for our baby, and then she miscarried. She was so devastated, I couldn't leave her and, not long after, she said she was pregnant again. This became a cycle and it destroyed me. I stayed with Melissa until just under a year ago. It'll be a year in December. I held on for so long because I let you go for her and I couldn't bear to think I made the wrong choice. I finally got tired of living a lie, of living in the shadow of what I lost because I was clinging to something that should've ended years before. I was so young, and so stupid." I reach out to take her hand in mine, shocked when she lets me. "I'm so sorry I hurt you. I'm so sorry I was a coward. I'm just—sorry. Nothing about what happened was right. I can't take back what I did and the things in my control that I ignored. I wish I could."

She licks her lips, searching my eyes, before she pulls her hand away and drops her eyes. "That's—a lot to take in."

"I know." I look at her, the weight of all the regrets heavy on my shoulders. I look back and think about how selfish I was. That selfishness caused me so much pain and grief. In the past seven years it's been a lot to come to terms with.

"I can understand the young part, our relationship started when it shouldn't have, neither of us able to see past the way we felt together. We both were young and foolish. I still can't help but wonder even after all you've told me—why not me? Why not at least talk to me?" She crosses her arms, the way she does when she's trying to protect herself, and starts walking again.

My face falls, my chest seizing as breathing becomes near impossible. "My parents weren't married when they had me, and they never were together. I was foolish enough to believe the small iota of feelings I had for Melissa before I met you was enough to make a relationship, a family, work. And then we experienced miscarriage after miscarriage. It was devastating. I think I wanted a baby so bad to make up for what I sacrificed, what I lost when I ended things with you."

Tilting my head up, I focus on the treetops as I fight back my emotions. Closing my eyes as snow starts to fall, I try to find my bearings. Small arms wrap around my waist, Allie's slender frame pressing into me. My arms automatically respond, holding her close as I look down at the crown of her head. Having her here, fitting into me in that perfect way, it feels so right. It's the piece that's been missing.

My arms fall away as she steps back, the devastation clear on her face. She shakes her head as I start to speak, turning to start walking again. Her eyes are downcast, her lashes glistening with melting snow. It pains me when I see a tear fall down her cheek and she turns her face away, hiding it from me.

If things had been different, this would be us right now. Except we would be holding hands and laughing together. Or I would be kissing her passionately in the snow, her favorite thing in the world. We might even have a baby to call our own. Instead, we're walking side by side with a respectable distance between us. Tears falling down her cheeks.

And even though I know it's wrong, I'm hoping some of those tears are falling for what we lost.

chapter
five

Allie

Brendan: I'm on my way home. I can't wait to see you.

Tugging the blanket more firmly around me, I clench my eyes shut and try to get my shit together. Everything Landon said to me today, the entire circumstances around our end and what he's gone through since that night, it's heavy on my mind.

I told Brendan I was meeting an old friend, that there was a heavy history and it was a chance to get some clarity. I'm still unsure what Landon wants from me and a part of me knows I should say goodbye and let myself move on, but another part of me, the part that's always felt this connection, this tether holding us together, baulks at that thought.

Keys rattle in the door, Brendan coming in with a

happiness that helps lift some of the burden I'm carrying. I know he could tell I was sad when we were texting earlier, he can always tell. Even when we first met, somehow he just saw something in me and knew I needed some lightness.

He leans over the back of the couch and blows a raspberry where my neck and shoulder meet, right where I'm ticklish. Giggling, my shoulder lifts reflexively, and I roll onto my back so I can find comfort in the gentle way he looks at me.

Before I can say anything, he lifts a bouquet of orchids from behind the couch, handing them to me. They're beautiful, purple and white with little hints of yellow.

"Oh, my goodness, they're gorgeous." I sit up, the first genuine smile I've had since I met Landon at lunch pulling at my lips as I hold the flowers to my nose and inhale the sweet fragrance. "What's the occasion?"

"You sounded so down in your text, I just wanted to see you smile. You should never be sad, Allie. You're too incredible." Brendan bends down once more, this time kissing me before smiling against my lips when I wrap my hand around the back of his neck.

We're both breathing heavily when he finally straightens, taking the flowers from my hands so he can put them in water.

"I was thinking we could go out tonight, do something fun," he suggests, his tone hopeful.

It was nice cuddling on the couch last night, I know we need more "us" time and I was could use the distraction. Besides, how long has it been since we went out on a date? I watch as Brendan fills a vase with water, arranges the flowers inside, and sets it on our kitchen table before turning to me.

Sitting up, the blanket falls around my waist. Brendan's eyes immediately look at my bare shoulder and

I can see his thoughts moving in a different direction. As much as I wish I could push thoughts of Landon aside, I can't bear the idea of being intimate with Brendan when another man is dominating the majority of my brain.

Grinning at him, I feed into the excitement of getting out and doing something else to occupy me. "Yeah! What do you have in mind?"

"It's a surprise." He grins at me when I groan jokingly, winking as he comes to pull me off the couch and wrapping me in his arms. "It'll be fun, I promise."

Forty-five minutes later, he's standing behind me, his hand wrapped around mine which is wrapped around the handle of an ax. My back is pressed against his chest, his cheek resting against the side of my head. He groans a little when I wiggle my ass, pressing it into his groin as we focus on the movement of our arms as we throw it, and miss the target entirely.

Turning to Brendan, I giggle, "This might be easier if we throw our own axes."

"Possibly, but I love the way you wiggle in excitement. Your way sounds like less fun, even if our axes might actually hit the target." He chuckles when I push him away playfully and pick up another ax. His hands go up in surrender as I glare at him, my lips twitching.

I watch him cross his arms, his eyes on me as I turn to face the target. Shifting around, I try to position my legs the way they taught us, sticking my tongue out for extra focus.

"I take it back; this way has its perks too." I glance behind me, rolling my eyes as he leans against the wall with a cocky grin on his face.

Refocusing on my task, I narrow my eyes and attempt to aim the ax at the center circle.

I release the ax and watching in complete shock as it hits the target right in the center. Throwing my arms in the air, I spin in a circle before turning and running at Brendan. He catches me, like I knew he would, and buries his face in my neck as I wrap my legs around his waist. This was exactly what I needed. Gushing, I pull back to meet Brendan's gaze. "This has been the perfect date night. I love you."

"I love you too, baby." His voice is hoarse, thick with emotion and it makes me pause. He looks like he's thrilled but sad at the same time. Then it dawns on me, we haven't been this affectionate in a long time, it's nice that we're focusing on getting out and doing things as a couple again.

Dropping my legs, I move to the side so Brendan can take his turn. As he picks up an ax I start heckling him when he hits the edge of the target. "C'mon, Scott, you can do better than that. Big strong man like you."

He scowls at me, his eyes laughing as he hands me an ax. "You lucked out. I doubt you'll hit that bullseye again."

Licking my lips, I slide my hand up and down the handle a couple of times, taunting him as I back away. With a grin, I turn around, center myself, and throw the ax. Right into the bullseye of the target.

Screaming in excitement, I dance in a circle, wiggling my hips. "Luck my ass."

Brendan stalks toward me, grabbing my hips and yanking me toward him. His lips crash onto mine, his desperate need for me causes a moan to slip out as I deepen the kiss, our tongues melding together.

"Want to get out of here?" He cups my cheeks, his erection pressing into me as he holds me close.

"We still have time left," I tease, a small smirk pulling at the corners of my lips.

He wraps his hand in my hair, kissing me again until we're both breathing heavily, before pressing his forehead to mine. "I don't care."

Licking my lips, I take his hand and lead him to the front counter to grab our belongings. We both need this, the closeness that's been lacking in our relationship for longer than I can identify.

"Let's go home." I barely recognize my voice, it's low and throaty, aroused.

I rest my hand on his thigh the entire drive home, only taking it away to get out of the car. As soon as the car is locked, we meet in front and his lips are on mine, devouring me as we stumble into the building, his hand smacking the button for the elevator before pressing me into the wall.

We fumble our way to our door, kissing and touching like it's the first time. I don't actually remember the last time I felt this aroused. Lately it's felt like intimacy is more of a chore, something to get done and then we can move on with our day. I can tell in the way Brendan is holding me, his arms wrapped around me so tight, that he needs this. He needs this closeness and I haven't been giving it to him.

Slamming our door shut behind us, I back down the hall leaving a trail of clothes. The way Brendan's eyes follow me, devouring my every movement, I crave that connection. I need it. I need to forget about anything else except the desire rolling off the man prowling after me. The amount of love in his eyes, it wraps around me in that comforting bubble.

Crawling up the bed, I sprawl out and tease my nipples, watching him as he loses the rest of his clothes and joins me on the bed. He holds himself above me, pressing down to kiss me as a thick "oh fuck" comes out on a deep moan.

Pressing my hand into his chest, I roll him onto his back and wrap my hand around his cock. Positioning myself over him, I sink down and twist my hips, watching how Brendan's eyes practically roll into the back of his head. I ride him until he slides his hands up my thighs, holds onto my hips and flips us back over. He grins down at me when I growl at him, but as he pins my legs up and pounds into me, I forget to be annoyed.

"Harder. Faster." My words come out as a whimpering beg, the deeper angle building me up until my body shudders with the magnitude of my release. I can't remember the last time I came so hard.

Our bodies are slick with sweat by the time he collapses next to me. Our chests rise and fall with our quickened breaths. Reaching over, I link my fingers with Brendan's, the sharp inhale of his breath sending pain through my chest. The fact that he's surprised any time I make a simple affectionate gesture speaks volumes about how little I've been showing him I care. Brendan has always been a physical guy, he thrives on physical intimacy. And not just sex, he loves everything, right down to something as simple as me running my fingers through his hair.

He squeezes my hand, rolling toward me and stroking my cheek. This is how we fall asleep, smiling at each other while holding hands.

chapter
six

Allie

Brendan is fast asleep next to me, his even breathing a soothing sound in the darkness. Yet sleep eludes me and I can't pinpoint why. Opening my eyes, I watch him sleep. His face is smooth, worry free. Instead of the usual comfort I get from being close to Brendan I feel— unsettled. Rolling to face away from him, I close my eyes and try to relax, try to find my calm.

This evening was some of the most fun Brendan and I have had in a long time. We haven't made time for a date night like that in months. I didn't realize how much I missed actually dating him until now. It's easy when you've been together for as long as we have to fall into a routine and take each other for granted.

Sometimes I forget how he made me laugh when no one else could. How he brought me out of my endless cycle of hurt, self-loathing, and regret at sacrificing my morals for someone who ended up breaking my heart.

We met less than a month after Landon had ended things and, despite my distance, he managed to weasel his way into my circle of friends a few months later. Less than a year later we went on our first date—a date that still hasn't been surpassed. He surprised me with zip lining in the mountains, something I'd always wanted to do.

It was his sense of humor, his ability to make me smile, and his adventurous spirit that made me fall in love with him. It's his kind heart and unwavering devotion that has kept us going for six years.

Brendan mumbles in his sleep, his still form relaxed. It's unusual for me to experience any form of insomnia, typically I fall asleep as soon as my head hits the pillow, but for whatever reason I just can't find that blissful moment when sleep pulls me in.

Flipping onto my back, I sigh in frustration. Reaching across to my nightstand, I grab my phone from the charger and tiptoe out of the room. Flipping on the TV, I turn the volume down and then check my phone.

> **Landon:** Thank you for giving me the chance to explain what happened.

Glancing at the time, I notice he texted me ten minutes ago.

Tucking my legs into my chest, I bite my lower lip as I type, my heart fluttering.

> **Me:** I think I needed to know what happened as much as you needed to tell me. Closure and all that.
>
> **Landon:** I hope I didn't wake you.
>
> **Me:** No, I couldn't sleep—if you didn't want to wake me, why did you text me at one in the morning?

Landon: I was watching a movie with my brothers. I started thinking about earlier and sent it before I thought about how late it was.

Me: What movie?

Landon: They wanted to watch *John Wick*.

Me: I haven't seen it.

Landon: It's pretty decent. We just switched off the TV and they went to bed.

Wrapping the blanket from the back of the couch around me, I smile as we continue to text back and forth, falling into the easy conversation that we enjoyed before he ended things.

Landon: Are you still coming for your appointment tomorrow after you're done work?

Me: Yeah, my neck is killing me. Especially after ax throwing this evening.

Landon: You went ax throwing?!

Me: Yeah, Brendan surprised me with a date night.

Unlike my previous texts, Landon doesn't text back right away. It's a splash of cold water, one that I think I needed. It's totally inappropriate to be talking to the man I used to love when Brendan is sleeping in the next room, especially when I'm sitting here like a giddy teenager talking to the boy she likes. A sick feeling replaces the butterflies in my stomach.

This is a slippery slope, one we've been on before, and I need to draw the line in the sand. My attraction for Landon is still there, so I need to be cautious and create firm boundaries if we are going to proceed with this friendship. A friendship I know I should probably say no to, but when my phone pings again, I eagerly look to see what he wrote.

Landon:	That sounds fun. I'd like to see you throw an ax.
Me:	I kicked ass.
Landon:	So—you're my last appointment of the day tomorrow. Maybe we can go for a drink after.
Me:	Okay.

Staring at my phone, I quickly type out a goodnight and shut it off. Rubbing my forehead, I shove up from the couch and rush back to bed.

Guilt fills me as I take in Brendan's peaceful form. He has a small smile on his face and his lips are moving, almost like he's having a conversation in his dream.

I feel one foot slip out from under me. If I'm not careful, my happy life is going to go up in flames.

Chimes announce my arrival at Landon's clinic. Locking the door behind me as he requested, I tuck my shoes under the rack and hang my stuff on the hooks. As I round the corner of the wall that separates the entryway from the rest of the clinic, I freeze at the sight before me. My mouth goes dry as I take in Landon, shirtless and doing pull-ups at a bar I didn't notice the last time I was here.

Landon as a nineteen-year-old was attractive. Landon as a twenty-six-year-old man is a work of art. His muscles flex as he lifts himself up before lowering back down at such a slow pace my own muscles ache in response.

Licking my lips, I tear my eyes away. My body feels too warm, energy pulsing through me as I fidget with the sleeves of my sweater until I hear his feet hit the floor with a thud.

This physical reaction to him is what lead us down the path of sneaking around. There is something irresistible about our connection.

Switching the song over, I laugh at the story Landon is telling me. My fingers are weaving their way through my hair as he locks eyes with me. We've been hanging out for several weeks now, but here in the confined space of my car, the tension is palpable.

By the time he finishes telling the story, I'm laughing so hard I can't seem to stop. He smiles at me, his eyes twinkling.

"Oh my God, just shut me up." Turning my head toward him, I gasp when his breath caresses my lips.

"Okay," he whispers, before crushing his lips to mine.

Taking a deep breath, I slowly turn to look at him again, still lost in the memory of our first kiss. Shoving away the memory, I meet his eyes. "Sorry, I'm a little early."

He gives me a wicked grin, his eyes locked on mine as he bends to nab his t-shirt from where it rests on a bench. Crossing my arms over my chest when he breaks eye contact to pull the shirt over his head, I grasp my elbows and hold on tight.

I can't believe the hold he still has on me. I should hate him, but the reality is, I hate myself. I hate the fact that I knowingly entered a relationship with someone who already had a girlfriend. I hate the fact that when he said he cared about me, that being with me had filled a missing hole and that he was going to end things with Melissa, I believed him. I hate that I fell for his pretty words, even though nine months passed and nothing changed.

What happened was an experience of naivety, but I'm not that twenty-year-old girl anymore. I believe him when he says he made a mistake he regrets, which is why we can move forward with being friends. I can forgive myself for our past mistakes and I will ignore the way he still manages to drive my hormones crazy. If not, I'll let the friendship go.

His hair is all mussed up when his head pops through the material, his arms flexing as he shoves them into the holes and adjusts the hem. It's not until he's striding toward me and the table I'm standing next to that I quit staring at his hair. The memories of running my fingers through it are strong and bring up too many emotions. I need to be better at blocking both the memories and the feelings they invoke.

"Hop up on the table." His deep voice is gruff, his eyes intent on mine as I do as he says. His fingers probe the muscles in my neck, steady and warm before he guides me through a series of motions. My head is swimming, barely able to follow through with his requests and all I can think about is how much I hope I'm miraculously better so I don't need to sit here with his hands on me anymore.

"You've been doing your exercises." His praise glides over me in a caress, a shiver running down my spine when he tweaks my ponytail the way he used to.

Shrugging, I give him a small smile, his affectionate gesture sending my stomach into my chest. "Well, my physical therapist told me that doing them would speed up my recovery time. He doesn't seem like a total idiot, so I listened."

His lips curl up in a lopsided smile. "Well, let's see if we can move me into the range of not being an idiot at all. Let's change up the exercises, your upper back is still too tight and I notice it's impacting your lower back and hips. Lie down, face up."

My back hits the vinyl, my eyes locked on the ceiling as he works with my hips and lower back. Curling my fingers, I press my nails into my palms to ground me. It doesn't work. My eyes flutter closed as I follow his warm touch.

The trampoline is cool on our backs as we stare at the stars. Everyone has left the party and we're finally able to relax, enjoy our time together without any pretenses. Landon's fingers leave trails of tingles as he runs them up and down my arm, my sharp inhalation filling the silence.

I bounce as Landon rolls onto his side.

"I love how responsive you are to my touch, the sounds you make are so sexy." He moans, his expression heated.

He presses into me, shifting until he's balancing on his forearms over me. We've been getting more intimate and I've been struggling with the fact that he's still with Melissa, but when we're together and he's touching me, that guilt fades just for the moment as I lose myself in the way he makes me feel.

When his lips brush against mine, I press up into him eager to connect our bodies even more. A moan slips out when he drops his weight onto me, his hands burying into my hair. I love the way his fingers massage my scalp in time with his kiss. Every part of me tingles, lost in the way he makes me feel.

"Stay with me. Please. I can't bear the thought of not holding you in my arms tonight."

I feel him standing above me before I hear him. "Did you fall asleep?" I pry open my eyes, blinking away the blurriness only to be met with his devastating smile, his expression teasing.

"No, just—thinking." Cringing at the throaty sound of my voice, I clear my throat and sit up, allowing him to help me off the table before stepping away in an effort to ignore the heat in his eyes.

For the next thirty minutes he runs me through a series of exercises, tweaking them until he's happy. My body is tired, my neck sore, by the time we wrap up.

Tilting my head side to side, I stretch it out. A little whoosh of air escapes when I feel Landon's large hands land on my shoulders, his thumbs kneading the muscles in my neck.

I'm putty in his hands as he works out the tension, relaxing to the point I'm wavering on my feet. That is until a moan escapes from my lips. His hands squeeze my shoulders a little tighter, his fingers pressing into my collarbone. I almost take a step back, a step that would press my back into his chest, but I manage to keep my feet planted.

I won't go through this again. I won't be responsible for another person getting hurt.

His breath is hot on my neck as he exhales, his hands falling away. I take two quick steps forward before turning to grab my jacket.

I'm completely bundled before I feel capable of meeting Landon's eyes, my face carefully impassive. He examines my expression, but doesn't comment as he brushes past me to unlock the door, holding it open for me.

A blast of cold air whips my hair around me, falling snow hitting me in the face as we exit the building and he locks up behind us. "Ugh. More frickin' snow."

He cocks his head to the side. "You love the snow. You used to talk about it all the time."

Hunching in on myself to fight the cold, I look up at him before glancing away as I answer, "I used to love it. I don't anymore."

He doesn't respond as we cross the road to an Irish pub I've never been in. McLaughlin's.

The door opens to a dimly lit room filled with music coming from a jukebox. Tables fill the center with booths lining the outer walls. The bar, lit with various beer signs, is against the wall closest to the entrance.

Landon leads me through the room to a secluded booth in the back corner. His hand brands my lower back as we walk. Even when it falls away, I can still feel the pressure, the heat.

He sits opposite me, resting his elbows on the table as he leans forward. "You disappeared on me fairly abruptly last night."

Tapping my fingers on the table, I lean back and meet his gaze. "Brendan was sleeping in the next room, sleeping and thinking I was in bed next to him, and there I was talking to you. It felt—familiar and wrong," I bite out, knowing my tone is harsh.

I won't lie to him, he'll see right through it, and if we're going to be friends, I need to be clear. The boundaries are already blurring and I can't seem to stop toeing the line. I know it's wrong, I know I would be upset if Brendan was behaving this way, yet here I am. That thought gives me pause and I pull out my cell to send him a quick text. He deserves to know where I am—and who I'm with.

Me: Hi. I know you're with clients, but I wanted to let you know Landon invited me for a drink. We're at McLaughlin's.

Sliding my phone back into its pocket, I resume tapping my fingers on the table.

"Would he be upset if you'd been talking to Blake or Dawn?" His tone is curious, but there is something else I can't quite figure out. He leans back, his knee brushing mine as he stretches out.

Glaring at him, I shift my knee away. "It's different, and you know it."

He sighs and scrubs a hand over his face. "You're right. I'm sorry. I'm being an ass, it's just so difficult being near you and knowing I can't brush your hair away from you face or hold your hand in mine." He laughs bitterly, shaking his head. "That's my fault and I hate myself for it."

It's at this moment that a server finally appears to take our drink orders. I don't look away from Landon, his form blurring a bit as he orders a margarita for me, my favorite, and a beer for himself.

Chewing on my lower lip, I look down for a moment until I feel strong enough to meet his steady gaze and hold it.

"Landon, please don't." Despite my best intentions, the words are laced with pain. Looking down, I whisper the words I can't say while staring into those piercing blue eyes. "Maybe this is too hard. I can't do this if it's going to undermine my relationship with Brendan. I can't do this if the conversation turns to topics he couldn't be present to listen to. I won't do it. I can't go through this again, I can't do that to him or myself."

"Shit, Allie, I'm sorry." His voice is hoarse, strained. "I can do this. I swear. I want you in my life. It's not too hard, we can be friends."

My knuckles turn white as I grip the edge of the table. He means the words he says, I know he does, but I can feel it in every fiber of my being that saying the words and meaning them is completely different from following through with the intent.

Releasing my grasp on the table, I smooth invisible wrinkles out as I lift my head once more. His gaze is pained, repentant. "I want you in my life too."

I do. I will cut him out if I need to, but the thought of losing him for a second time is so painful, I need to close my eyes. Why is life so cruel? Things didn't work back then and now we're in a situation where both of us are going to get hurt, it's not a matter of if, but when. The feelings between us are too intense and my heart still has cracks in it from the first time.

He sags in relief, giving me a lopsided grin. I can tell by

the look he shoots in my direction that his heart still hurts too.

For the longest time I thought it was one-sided, but now I know better. That night we were both wrecked and yet here we are, repeating history. Both of us know it, neither of us strong enough to stop it. But maybe I am strong enough, maybe I can keep the boundaries. We're older, wiser, and I like to think I'm capable of controlling myself.

Our drinks arrive and we fall into easy conversation as one drink turns into two, the awkwardness fading into the background. I don't know how much times passes, but our glasses are empty and the pub is near empty when my phone dings with a text.

> **Brendan:** You sure are beautiful when you smile like that.

Snapping my head up, I search the bar, my smile becoming slightly forced when I see him meandering through the tables toward us. I automatically glance at Landon when Brendan slides into the booth next to me, his arm wrapping around my shoulders as he pulls me in for a hug and a kiss.

It's not possessive or jealous, it's just Brendan, and yet—him just showing up puts a weird feeling in my chest.

I meet Landon's gaze once more, the introduction falling from my lips when I see the strained smile on his face. Clearing my throat, I pull my lips into a bright smile. "Brendan, this is Landon. Landon, this is my boyfriend, Brendan."

Despite my history with Landon, Brendan's smile is friendly as he reaches across the table to shake Landon's hand. I filled him in this morning on everything up to this point, and in true Brendan fashion, he was completely understanding and supportive.

My heart pounds in my chest as two different aspects

of my life collide, my ears ringing as Brendan strikes up a conversation with Landon about his work. Brendan sips his beer, his eyes light with interest. He seems completely oblivious to the tension surrounding us as I shoot furtive glances across the table.

This is what I was worried about. This feeling of doing something that I shouldn't. This time the excitement is gone, because even with the guilt, sneaking around with Landon always had an element of excitement. The thrill of doing something I know is wrong isn't there, at least I know I've learned something.

I sag in relief when the bartender rings the bell announcing last call. Brendan glances down at me in confusion over my physical reaction to the bell, while Landon throws a bunch of bills onto the table and slides out of the booth.

The silence is awkward as we walk out together, pausing by Brendan's car. With a lingering kiss and a promise from me that I'll be home soon, Brendan turns to Landon and shakes his hand again.

"It was nice to meet you." His voice is genuine, one hundred percent Brendan.

Landon glances down to the firm grasp Brendan has on his hand before giving him a small smile. "Likewise."

They drop hands and Brendan slides into his car and shuts the door. As he drives away, I hustle to my car with my head dropped low, a heavy weight settling over me. Landon creates a wall of heat in the chill of the night air as he walks me to my car.

My skin is tingling and my heart is pounding while I try to think of something to say that will fill the silence but is safe.

"He doesn't like me," Landon says in a quiet voice before I can come up with something to say. He glances down at me as we reach my car, waiting for my response.

My car beeps as I unlock it and he opens the door for me, but I don't get in.

I sigh. "Brendan likes everyone. He just wonders why we're hanging out after what happened, he knows who you are and he knows about our history, I filled him in this morning. I told you, I'm not lying to him." I move to slide into my car, but I'm suddenly pulled into the warmth of Landon's arms, his massive size enfolding me. I hug him back, sinking into it before I drag myself away.

"Goodnight, Landon."

Getting into my car, I shut the door without a word and start the engine. A breath whooshes out of me as I grip the steering wheel. Conflicting emotions wage war inside my chest the entire drive home.

It *was* unusual for Brendan to show up randomly, he's never done that when I've been out with friends. It means he either felt I needed support, or he's jealous for the first time in six years. Guilt sinks its vicious claws into me because I know that it would be my fault if jealousy drove the impromptu visit. I know that Brendan wouldn't be jealous unless he felt our relationship, our happiness, was being threatened.

chapter
seven

Landon

It's been four days since Brendan showed up at the pub, four days since I saw Allie hug and kiss another man. In those four days, I haven't been able to think about anything else. Watching them together was one of the most painful things I've ever experienced. A small taste of what Allie went through with me and Melissa.

It was eye opening, the fact that she trusted me and dealt with my bullshit for nine months, I wouldn't get away with that now. We were both so young, but the connection was real—is real—losing her was probably the biggest loss of my life.

I've felt short of breath from the moment he sat down and I still feel like I can't get enough air. Seeing the live version as opposed to pictures online, it was complete torture.

It's obvious he loves Allie, there's no misreading the

way he looks at her. And as much as it pains me to admit, she loves him back. There are years of time spent and affection built on their foundation, whereas we had nine months of intense falling.

A part of me was hoping he wasn't good enough for her, that he didn't appreciate her or was uninterested in the relationship. Scoffing, I shake my head. Only an idiot would have Allie and not appreciate her.

Melissa is laughing at something Tyler said, something I probably should've heard, but all I can focus on is Allie. Her hips sway to the music as she dances with her friends, her smile making my heart beat a little faster. I love her smile. It makes my day better every time I see it.

She hasn't noticed me sitting with Melissa and our friends, she's distracted by the music and how much fun she's having. I should turn away, but I can't find the will.

Someone kicks me under the table. Jerking my head over, I see Ty glaring at me.

He mouths, "Dude, what the hell are you doing?"

Shaking my head, I ignore him and scan the room in an attempt not to be so obvious. As my gaze glides over Allie, I meet her hazel eyes. Eyes that look sad as she glances at where Melissa is tucked right against me.

I recall the feeling of my stomach dropping when Allie turned her back to me, returning her attention to her friend and thinking, *"I need to fix this soon or I'm going to lose her."* Wasn't that the truth. Forcing my thoughts to the present, I switch the plastic bag I'm holding to my other hand, pull my phone from my pocket and scroll through the messages from my brothers.

Kellan: Where are you? I half-expected you to be on the couch with a pint of ice cream in hand with the amount of moping you've been doing.

Me:	I'm finally returning those shoes. And I'm not moping.
Josh:	You're moping.

Rolling my eyes, I put my cell back in my pocket. They're not wrong, I have been moping. I never stopped loving Allie, even when I was trying to make things work with Melissa, my heart was never in it. Allie's held my heart since the moment we first shared a table in a crowded coffee shop. It doesn't matter how many years have passed, I've never been able to let her go.

Part of me thought we would get our second chance when I literally ran into her, and now I'm stuck in the friend-zone, because I wasn't lying, I will take her any way I can get her even though it's painful.

I consider myself a level-headed guy. I don't cling to things unnecessarily, moving on when things don't work. With Allie though, I don't know how to turn off these feelings and I honestly don't think I want to.

Then I think about the future and what friendship with her means. I don't know if I can watch her walk down the aisle to marry Brendan. Or watch her stomach swell with his child. I don't know if I can reasonably meet someone with her in my life when I'm pining over the future I know would've been mine if I hadn't ended things with her. It would have been mine. It should've been mine.

I was so damn stupid, and I know I was nineteen, but I shouldn't have sacrificed a relationship with the woman I loved to make something work with a woman I didn't. The moment my lips first touched Allie's I should have ended things with Melissa.

Shoulda. Woulda. Coulda. Everything is clear in hindsight.

Growling, I leave the store. I'm so lost inside my own head that my entire time here at the mall is a blur. Running a hand through my hair, I shake my head, and plow right into the person in front of me.

"Shit, I'm sorry—Allie." Her gorgeous hazel eyes peer up at me, looking bemused.

"You seem to have a habit of crashing into me." She takes a step back, but her smile is friendly and unguarded. The only sign that she's as impacted by how close we were is the dilation of her pupils.

"Apparently." She smiles at the humor in my voice as we move aside so we're not blocking people hustling around us. She looks beautiful, her hair in loose curls around her shoulders, her lips tilting in an easy smile.

"I had some last-minute gifts come up that I needed to buy, and so here I am. It was foolish to think I was done with my Christmas shopping. Would you like to join me?"

I finally notice the bags in her hands and reach out to take them from her as I nod.

"Yeah." We start walking as she checks the list in her hand. I glance at her, before trying to sound nonchalant as I say, "You've been pretty quiet for the last four days."

I know I'm transparent as soon as she glances sideways at me, her lips twitching.

"I know. Work's been intense. We finally hired a new developer and we're briefing her on the park we've been planning. We want to ensure everything is set for spring. Especially since it was supposed to be completed already." She presses a hand into my side to nudge me toward a bookstore.

I follow her inside as she wanders through the aisles. "That must be a relief."

"It is, but I don't want to talk about work." She makes an adorable face, stopping at a rack to flip through a selection of notebooks. She pauses in her perusal to look at me. "I wasn't avoiding you."

I chuckle as she returns her focus to the notebooks,

moving along the shelf until she sees something she likes. "I didn't ask."

"Didn't you?" She flips through the pages of a book she's picked up before setting it back on the shelf. She turns to look at me, adjusting the strap of her purse on her shoulder. Her words are quiet, but hit me straight in the gut. "If our roles were reversed, that's what I would've been thinking."

She takes the notebook she was looking at and, with one last glance at me, heads toward the front counter.

Following her, we're quiet until we're back out into the bustling crowd of the mall. She's right, I did think she was avoiding me, and I don't think she's being entirely truthful when she says she wasn't. I think she's scared of our lingering feelings toward each other and the fact that life seems to be bringing us down a familiar path. I don't know how to reassure her, other than show her we won't put ourselves in that position again.

"Your birthday is coming up. What do you have planned?" We stop to grab some coffee, sitting at one of the small round tables overlooking the fountains in the center of the mall. It's oddly reminiscent of when we met, except neither of us are attempting to study anything but each other.

"Ugh. I don't want to do anything, it's supposed to snow all weekend and I just want to hibernate the whole time, but Brendan is insisting on planning a party." The smile pulling at her lips takes away the bite of her words.

I never got to celebrate a birthday with her. Never got to plan a gift or something fun to do. Another thing we missed out on and this time I get to be a bystander in her life. It fills me with an annoying sense of melancholy. I feel like an emo teenager, not a grown ass man.

As we sit and drink coffee, we discuss our plans for the holidays and weird traditions our families have. I've spent so much time fighting my attraction, I forgot how much fun we have when we're hanging out and chatting.

After we finish our coffee we get through the rest of Allie's list before she drags me into a hat store. She disappears to the back and when she reappears she's wearing the most ridiculous hat I've ever seen. It's lime green with actual metal locks and feathers, a weird combination, and one of those nets that covers half her face.

"Who would buy that?" We laugh, much to the annoyance of the staff member passing us.

I see a hipster version of a lumberjack hat, snag it off the shelf and plop it on my head while striking a pose. Allie disappears again, returning with what looks like a *Muppet* on her head.

"I always pass this store and laugh at some of the weird hats, but never come in." She giggles as we find different ones to try on. She looks adorably sexy in all of them, her cheeks flushed with happiness.

After thirty minutes of playing, we leave the store with huge smiles on our faces. Allie checks the time, sending a quick text before she reaches for her bags. "I better go. I had so much fun shopping this afternoon."

"I did too. It was nice to get away from my brothers." I roll my eyes, smiling. "I'll walk you to your car."

She grins as we leave, chatting about things we pass as we walk. After we reach her car and her purchases are safely stowed away, I give her a quick hug before opening her door. "I hope you have a great night. If it's not too weird, I would love to come celebrate your birthday with you and your friends."

She beams at me. "I'd love that."

chapter
eight

Allie

Picking up my phone, I open my calendar and scan my day. Joining Brendan in the kitchen, I look at him and grimace. "I have six meetings today, six. It's insane. And the very first one, we get to sit down with our investors and present our new timeline while simultaneously asking for more money. Fun, right?"

Shaking my head, I smile, because as much as my job can be stressful, and six meetings will lead to coffee breaks spent at my desk, I love my job. I couldn't ask for better coworkers, and I couldn't be more invested in making our town a better place.

Sitting down, I devour the oatmeal waiting for me. Brendan's oatmeal is homemade, with cinnamon, chunks of apple, and he even slices a banana to add to mine.

"At least things are moving forward now." He sits next to me, his tone encouraging.

"Yeah, that eases some of my frustrations. I hate being stagnant." Pausing when my phone dings, I see Landon sent me a text.

It's a photo of PeeWee laying on his back with a stuffed bear tucked in between his front legs. He's fast asleep, his tongue lolling out the side of his mouth.

Chuckling, I quickly type out an "aww," before continuing my thought. "It's the worst feeling."

When I glance at Brendan, he has a faraway look in his eyes and his brows are furrowed. He looks worried, like he's carrying a hefty burden.

When my phone pings again, the furrow deepens. He hasn't said anything about my friendship with Landon, and our relationship has been better lately, so I'm not sure if I'm reading too much into his look. I've been trying so hard to show him I care, I don't know what else I can do.

Ignoring the text, I flip my phone over and glance over at him. He's stirring his oatmeal over and over, lost in thought.

When he feels my gaze, he meets my eyes and his expression clears. "So, we need to talk about the elephant in the room." He smiles, pushing his half-finished bowl of oatmeal away.

My heart picks up, but his expression is teasing, so I tilt my head confused. "Elephant?"

"Your birthday. I've already confirmed with Blake and Dawn. Monique is out of town, but your parents are free. I'm still waiting to hear from my family." He takes a sip of his coffee, watching my face. I try to give him a look of excitement, but I'm sure he sees right through it. "Is there anyone I'm missing?"

Chewing on my lower lip, I release it and take a deep

breath. It's asking a lot, but maybe this will be a good thing, because one thing Landon never did was put me and Melissa in the same room, maybe it would have created a different situation, there would have been more of a connection and I would've been able to walk away. "I'd like to invite Landon, if that's okay with you?"

I don't release his gaze, but he stands up to go dump out the rest of his breakfast into the compost bucket. His voice is a little sharper than usual when he finally replies, his gaze locked on the backsplash above the sink, "Of course. It's your birthday party."

I watch him. I know Brendan would never tell me I can't be friends with someone, he's not that type of guy, but I also need him to be honest with me about where he's at, and right now, I can't really read what he's feeling.

He saw me after Landon ended things. He knows how hurt I was and he knows how much effort it took for me to trust him. Things have gone well for us over the last six years, we haven't hit any major bumps in the road.

Standing, I set my bowl on the counter and wrap my arms around him, pressing myself into his back. I talk into his shirt, careful of how to approach this. "Regardless, I know you're not entirely comfortable with our friendship."

He turns to face me, pressing his lips to my forehead. We stand together for a few minutes, my arms tight around him before he leans away.

I can't imagine how I would react if I was in his shoes, maybe I would be okay with it, maybe I wouldn't, but the part of me that knows I'm not being fair to Brendan is overshadowed by the connection Landon and I share.

If Brendan tells me right now he's uncomfortable, I will listen. If he tells me right now he wants me to cut ties with Landon, I will.

The idea of not seeing Landon again is painful, only

eased by the fact Brendan will never tell me I can't spend time with someone, no matter who it is.

"I don't know him. Maybe having him at your party is a good idea." He sounds upbeat, but I can see the wheels turning in his head. I can't help but wonder what he's thinking, but maybe once he has time to think it through, he will fill me in.

I grin at him, running my fingers through his hair as I press a light kiss to his lips. "I love you."

"I love you too."

Glancing at the time, I quickly jot Landon's number down before putting my coat on. Brendan comes to the door, kissing me before I leave.

I try not to overthink the fact that Brendan is calling him, so I busy myself with searching for funny pictures to send to Brendan throughout the day.

He's been there for me every single day, even when he had nothing to gain.

I'm staring at the wooden desk in front of me, avoiding the pitying gazes of my classmates. I look like I was in a fight, the bruises under my eyes from not sleeping more pronounced with each day that goes by.

I'm shattered. I made the mistake of stalking Landon's social media profiles last night and he looks—happy. There weren't any photos of him with Melissa, but she was commenting on them like crazy. It sent me spiraling. I haven't been able to sleep well in four months. My dreams full of different scenes playing out, all mocking me for my foolishness.

Movement in the seat next to me catches my eye. Glancing to my side, I see Brendan glance at me and smile when he meets my gaze. He's sat next to me every day since the beginning of this semester.

We've worked on a few projects together and have become friends. Somehow, he manages to make me smile.

He holds up a finger before leaning down to dig through his bag. I watch him, curious, but I can't see what he's doing.

"Hey, I have something for you." He smiles at me, his expression nervous as he pulls his hands out from behind his back and presents me with a stuffed penguin.

It's incredibly soft, the pads of my fingers smoothing the fluffy material. Looking up at him, I cradle it to my chest and smile. Once again, he just knew today would be a day I needed cheering up. How does he always know?

"Thank you, Brendan. I love him."

A weight lifts from my chest as I hug the penguin to me for the rest of class. We stand, Brendan asking if I want to have lunch with him. Nodding, I follow him out into the crowded hall, feeling a little better than I did this morning.

Landon

My phone rings, a number I don't recognize popping up on the screen.

"Hello?" I answer with caution, my finger poised over the hang-up button in case it's a solicitor and scam.

"Hi, Landon. This is Brendan, Allie's boyfriend." His voice is confident, steady. Like he doesn't care at all that he's calling her ex.

Pausing, I take a deep breath and try for the same level of nonchalance. "What can I do for you?" I'm pretty sure I failed when my voice comes out more wary than effortless.

"I was just calling you to invite you to Allie's birthday

party this weekend. It's low-key because Allie doesn't like anything big, but we'd like for you to come if you're free. I know it's short notice." He stresses the we, the only sign he's not totally on board with me being there. I'm sure part of this is a ploy to evaluate the situation, because that's what I'd be doing.

"I'm free. Thanks for the invite." This time my voice is more casual.

He rattles off their address and declines my offer to bring something.

The entire conversation takes less than two minutes but as I stare at the ended call, for the first time I doubt whether I want to go. An hour was torture watching them, how am I going to manage for an entire evening?

Grabbing PeeWee's leash, I take him for a quick walk before I leave for work. He bounces his way through the park near my house, barking at squirrels and sniffing through the snow.

Glancing at my phone, I look at the last text I sent Allie. The one she hasn't responded to.

> **Me:** Do you remember that time we were listening to music in your car, and you couldn't stop laughing? I hope for your birthday you get as much laughter as that night.

Shaking my head, I shove my phone back into my pocket.

"What are you doing?" My voice is loud in the empty park as I berate myself. That was the night of our first kiss. The one that sent us spiraling. No wonder she didn't respond.

Muttering to myself about what an ass I am, I walk PeeWee back home and head to work.

Things with Allie, they are what they are. I either need to accept them, or let her go.

chapter
nine

Allie

Stepping back from the mirror, I check myself out. Despite my makeup and hair being done up, I can see the strain over this evening written all over my face. I'm glad Landon is coming tonight, but I also know continuing to mesh my past with my present isn't going to be easy.

My stomach jumps when I hear voices out in the living room. Listening intently, I hear Blake's loud laugh, followed by Dawn's soft voice. The churning of my stomach settles a little, my friends will make a good buffer for when Landon arrives. Brendan was incredibly supportive of him coming, but he's been quieter than normal today.

Why am I putting us through this? It's a question I've been consumed with since Brendan said that Landon was coming tonight. I feel pulled in two different directions and I hate that even at twenty-eight I still don't seem to have the strength to cut Landon out of my life.

Taking a deep breath, I open the door and smile as my friends rush at me.

"Happy Birthday!" they say in unison, enveloping me in a group hug.

"Thank you." I peer over their shoulders and watch Brendan disappear into the kitchen before whispering, "So, Landon is coming tonight."

Dawn's eyes widen in shock as a slow smirk crosses Blake's face. "You sure don't like to live a simple life, hey?"

They know what's been going on, every single detail right down to my struggle with the lingering attraction, but this will be the first time they see the dynamic for themselves.

Dawn pulls a bottle of wine from her purse with a glance over at where Brendan is laying out all the food he prepared. "I think we better crack this bad boy now." She grimaces empathetically.

Dawn is trying her best to be supportive of my decision to keep Landon in my life, but I know she disapproves. In her opinion, Brendan is better than Landon in every way. We've talked at length about the potential consequences this path will lead to, including damaging my relationship with Brendan permanently. I think she's going to the extreme, because I promised myself that wouldn't happen.

Blake, on the other hand, is more supportive. She believes that Landon came back into my life for a reason and I need to find out what that reason is.

Whatever the situation, I spent the entire day contemplating telling Landon tonight it's too difficult to be friends with him, but every time I held that conversation in my head, it hurt so much, I couldn't even get the words out. So, for right now, I'm going to see if we can make it work. Something in me is so connected to him, I feel more whole with him in my life, and maybe this will work out in a way no one expects.

"God, yes. Wine sounds like a great idea." I'm just passing the door when a knock echoes through the room. Blake and Dawn continue toward the kitchen with raised brows, while Brendan pauses in his task and looks at the door, his brows furrowing before he goes back to what he was doing.

Sure enough, Landon stands on the other side. He looks devastatingly handsome in dark wash jeans and a pale blue button-down shirt. A pretty green package with a purple bow sits in his hand.

I can't help the smile that forms when he gives me a crooked grin. Moving aside, I feel three sets of eyes on us as he comes inside the condo.

"Happy Birthday." His voice is low, husky. His words just for me. "Don't open this yet, save it for later."

I take the gift from him with quiet thanks and set it off to the side, away from the others. After a quick round of reintroductions as Landon has met everyone, we're soon congregated around the counter picking at the food.

Blake strikes up a conversation with Landon as I wander over to where Brendan is standing, looking through the pantry. Tucking myself into his side, I pull him down so I can kiss his cheek. "Why don't we call this good, you know my mom will bring a ton of food. Come visit."

I fold my hand into his and tug on his arm. We join Dawn at the counter and she strikes up a conversation with Brendan about work. Smiling at her gratefully as he relaxes and starts talking animatedly, I snack on the delicious treats he made as they chat. He grins at me when I make a duck beak from two *Pringles*.

I lean into him as he wraps his arm around me, trying to pay attention to what he and Dawn are discussing. Dawn is a real estate agent and they love talking about the housing market.

My skin warms, and I glance up to see Landon looking at me over Blake's shoulder. He gives me a cocky grin that sends a shiver down my spine. Warmth pools in my stomach as he winks at me before returning his attention to Blake.

Snagging a piece of broccoli, I smile around it as we meet eyes again and he makes a face at me. When Landon came back into my life I didn't know if I would still like him the way I did before. As soon as I saw him, I knew the physical attraction was still there, but I had no idea this playful friendship would pick right back up.

Time has the potential to change people, and while we're both more mature and have more life experiences under our belts, at the root of it Landon is still the same guy I fell for so long ago. There is an easiness there that we fell right back into, that same easiness that made me fall for him in the first place.

Landon ducks down, picking me up and tossing me in the pool. When my head breaks the surface, I splash at him only to realize he's nowhere in sight.

Squeaking when a hand grabs my ankle, I'm pulled below the surface again.

This time we come up together and an all-out splash war starts until we're laughing so hard I almost snort.

Our laughter dies though when the alarm on his phone goes off. It's our signal that he needs to leave. The reminder that he still hasn't ended things with Melissa looms over me.

Ducking under the water, I swim away from him so I can pull myself together. I've made my bed and now I need to lie in it. I've fallen for him and the thought of walking away now hurts too much. I need to have faith in him and us, faith that he will follow through with his promises.

Looking down, I fight back the question of "what if," the one that's usually followed by the self-deprecating "why not me?" We're friends. And I'm glad to have our friendship back, because that's what our romantic relationship had been built on, but there's a part of my heart that yearns for more and the side of guilt that comes along with it is making me crazy.

Glancing over at Brendan, I watch him talking with Dawn while reminding myself what I love about him.

He's steadfast and loyal. Kind and funny. He loves me with a dedication that makes me feel safe and secure. He's everything I ever wanted in a partner. Brendan and I have fun, we laugh together, and things just—flow. It's easy, predictable.

There is nothing he wouldn't do to make me smile. He's open to trying new things, even when it might not be up his alley. And he always, always talks to me about everything. I have never met someone as honest as Brendan. Ever.

Watching them, I take advantage of their preoccupation as they discuss work and slip out to the balcony to get some fresh air. It's the perfect opportunity to clear my head as I struggle with the feeling that despite all of that, it's still not enough.

When I hear the sliding glass door open and shut again, I don't turn around. I know it's him. He leans against the railing next to me, the small wrapped package in his hand.

"Happy Birthday." Landon's voice is low, the rumble sending shivers down my spine as he hands me the gift.

"Thank you." My voice is soft as I look down at the pretty green and purple covering the gift.

He takes the ribbon and paper from me as I unwrap it,

before opening a plain black box. Nestled inside is a glass snowflake necklace. Underneath is a certificate of authenticity from a local glassblower, it's one of a kind. My throat catches at the thoughtfulness of this gift.

I feel him watching me, but I can't tear my eyes away from the gorgeous snowflake. It's not until he tucks a stray strand of hair behind my ear that my attention is stolen. Glancing over my shoulder, I sag in relief when everyone is still occupied.

"Allie—" He pauses until I meet his gaze. "Don't let one moment steal a lifetime of joy. Don't give anyone that power."

Dropping my eyes back to the necklace, I put together the deeper meaning of this gift. Landon knows me so well, he knows why I hate the snow.

Blinking back tears, I look back up at him and whisper my thanks. He smiles, it's filled with regret, longing, and sadness.

Unable to stop myself, I clutch the box to my chest and wrap my free arm around him. His familiar scent envelopes me and his arms wrap around me and hold me to him. This hug feels like so much more than a simple thank you.

When we turn to go back inside, my gaze meets Brendan's. He's just on the other side of the sliding glass door, his expression tight as he forces a smile to his face. Walking inside, I head straight into his arms and hold him tightly as I attempt to reassure him of something I'm not even certain of.

Landon

I'm exhausted by the time I get home. Spending the night watching Allie with Brendan, seeing the way her parents adore him and the way he gets along so well with her friends, it was eye opening.

All the things I want, all the things I could have had, and I got to watch someone else experience it. Torture. I knew what I was signing up for when I suggested being friends, but the ache in my chest right now feels like my heart was ripped out and set out on display.

Despite the longing, I tried to show Allie I could be her friend, and I think I succeeded. Having her back in my life has filled a hole and no matter how difficult it is, I would rather be able to talk to her and spend time with her than lose her again.

Kellan looks up from the couch as I drop down next to him, running my hand through my hair.

"Rough night?" His tone is colored with amusement.

"Shut up." I scowl at him.

PeeWee jumps up on the couch, squirming as he tries to lick my face in greeting. Scratching behind his ears, I lean my head back onto the couch and look over at Kellan.

"You don't get what it's like. I've never felt this way about anyone, and I doubt I ever will again. Having her back in my life means the world to me, but it's shitty that it's not in the way I want." He sobers at the tortured tone to my voice. The rawness that makes my entire body ache.

"Dude. *You* walked away from *her*. Are you shocked that someone else snapped her up?" He arches a brow and crosses his arms.

"I was a fucking kid!" I scowl at him, picking up a pillow and clenching it in my fist. "And obviously I'm not surprised. You just can't understand because you've never felt the way I do about Allie. She's a once in a lifetime kind of love." My voice raises, my defenses kicking in. I don't need him to remind me that I made the decision that led to this. I remind myself of it every damn day.

Tucking PeeWee under my arm, I shove up from the couch and head into my room. I set him on his pillow before brushing my teeth, stripping to my boxers, and throwing myself on my bed.

Picking up my iPad, I scan through emails and check my calendar for the next week. Allie and I have our final physio appointment this week. She's healed fast because of her diligence to completing the exercises at home. She will need to keep up on them, but she won't need my guidance anymore.

The selfish part of me wants to disregard her relationship and make a move, but the other part of me, the rational part, knows that would be a mistake. Her name glares out at me, so I toss my iPad aside and pick up the book I started a few days ago.

Ten years ago, I hated reading, but now it's my only escape when my head is being bogged down with things outside of my control. As I immerse myself into the fantastical world, I feel the tension start to release from my shoulders.

Between the black ink on the page taking me away to a different time and place, and PeeWee's soft snores, I finally forget everything else.

When I drop the book onto my face for the second time, I know it's time to set it aside and try to get some sleep. Picking up my phone to check the time, I notice that Allie sent me a text eight minutes ago. It's two in the morning, but the sleepiness I was feeling dissipates just by seeing her name on my screen.

Allie: You up?

Me: Yeah, I was reading, but I think I'll end up with a bruise if I drop my book on my face again.

Allie: Lol, it's happened to me.

There's a pause before she starts typing again. The little dots appearing and disappearing a few times before another text comes through.

Allie: I just wanted to thank you again for the necklace and the words. What happened that night—it made me angry and sad for a long time. I don't know if I ever really let it go, but lately things are just getting a little clearer. I sat outside on our balcony after everyone left, bundled up and just enjoying the snow. I was finally honest with myself and found a lot of clarity that I've been missing. I will always be grateful to you for that.

I reread that last sentence at least five times trying to read between the lines. She starts typing again before I can formulate a response.

Allie: I'm going to be turning my phone off for a few days, I have a lot of work to do and I need to disconnect for a while. I'll see you at my physio appointment this week. Goodnight, and thank you again for coming to my party this evening. I'm so glad you were there.

With a sinking feeling, I set my phone on my nightstand and turn to face my wall. Her text feels like more than a goodbye for now, it feels like a goodbye forever.

chapter
ten

Allie

Brendan has been out all day, so I spent my time cleaning the condo and prepping dinner for him for once. My birthday party was eye opening. Seeing my two worlds mesh into one. I watched how my family interacted with Brendan, having rarely interacted with Landon, they were friendly, but the connection with Brendan is deeper.

Seeing the sad look on Brendan's face when I came in from the balcony after receiving the snowflake, it hit me how difficult it is for him to know I'm friends with someone who held—holds—so much power over my heart. And it hurt. It hurt knowing I was doing that to him. This constant internal battle has become too much and I know I need to make a decision, because the other thing I realized last night is that I'm not capable of only having friendly feelings toward Landon.

Opening the oven, I slide the roast pan inside and set the timer.

My cell rings as I turn on the water to clean up the dishes, pausing, I glance over and relax when I see it's Dawn.

"Hey, Dawn. How's it going?" Smiling, I tuck my phone between my ear and shoulder, and set about loading the dishwasher.

"It's okay. Look, I need to be candid with you." Her voice is off, abrupt, and not Dawn-like.

"Okay. Are you okay?" I pause what I'm doing and lean against the counter.

"Not really. Allie, I ran into Brendan when I ran out to get coffee, and we talked. About you. About him. About Landon." Her tone is low, and I know she's not happy with me. "He's tortured, Allie. What are you doing to him? Either make the decision to be committed to your relationship because you want to, not out of guilt. Or let him go. He loves you, he feels that things are different. And you're not being fair."

"Hold on a second. I've been trying to be more attentive. Trying to spend more quality time with him." Her words hurt, but they're true. I'm a little annoyed that Brendan went to Dawn to complain about it instead of coming to me, like he should. It's not fair, I know he would come to me if he felt like it would make a difference.

"He feels like it's out of guilt. I know you're getting defensive because you know what he's saying is true. So, what are you going to do? He deserves more. And quite frankly, so do you and Landon. This isn't good for you or for Brenden. I thought you learned that the last time." She grows quiet, her voice a little thicker when she whispers, "I know the connection you feel with Landon is deep, but you've been with Brendan for six years. Respect that, respect him, because he would never treat you the way you're treating him."

"I know." I sigh, my eyes burning. "I've been thinking about it since last night, and all day today. I'm sorting through it, everyone just needs to give me some time."

"Don't take too much time, you don't have that luxury." She says goodbye and we hang up, the phone blurry as I stare at it.

I hear the front door open, so I shake it off, take a sip of wine, and pop my head out of the kitchen to greet Brendan.

"Just in time. Dinner is ready, and I bought *Guardians of the Galaxy Volume Two,* I know we missed it in theaters because of me, so I thought we could shut our phones off, have a nice dinner, and then watch both movies back to back." I smile at him, and then duck back into the kitchen to set the table.

I'm setting the salad I made on the table when he strides toward me and pulls me into his arms. Sinking into him, I breathe in the fresh scent of winter air and the soap from his shower this morning. We cling to each other, both knowing something needs to change, but neither of us sure what that means.

He breathes in deep, before brushing my hair to the side and kissing my neck. "That sounds like a perfect evening."

For the first time in a long time, neither of our phones are sitting next to us as we eat. Instead, we just talk. We talk about books we're reading or want to read. We talk about funny things we noticed over the day.

It's nice, and as we eat, I think about how much I would miss this if it was gone.

"I had coffee with Dawn today," Brendan mentions as we're cleaning up, my hand pauses on the lid of the plastic container I'm closing. I don't want him to know she called me.

I press the lid down and put the container in the fridge before turning to smile at him as I shut the door. "Oh nice. I've been meaning to text her and Blake to make plans for this week."

He looks a little disappointed, like he wishes I would ask what they talked about, but I know if I ask he will tell me, and I'm not ready to have that conversation yet.

Instead, I grab some popcorn and fill the air popper while he gets the movie ready. Turning off the lights, we settle on the couch next to each other. I shift over and curl into his side, needing to give *us* one hundred percent of my focus.

Every so often Landon will pop up in my head, but I shove him away and focus on relaxing. I feel Brendan's eyes on me throughout the movie, I can feel the weight of his conversation with Dawn. I don't doubt she told him he needs to talk to me, that we need to figure out what we're doing, but I'm choosing to leave the discussion alone for now. We're not ready to make any decisions, or, I should say, I'm not ready.

chapter
eleven

Allie

Hanging up, I turn and smile at Brendan. We just finished eating breakfast in bed, enjoying a leisurely morning together. "I officially have the day off tomorrow. What do you want to do?"

Shutting down my cell, I put it in my nightstand. Out of sight, out of mind. Brendan leans over and wraps his arms around me, the familiar comforting scent of his shampoo easing the anxiety I feel over turning my phone off.

My mind has been entirely focused on us and figuring out where we go from here for the past thirty-six hours. I need to figure out exactly how I feel about my relationship and the only way I can fairly do that is to give Brendan one hundred percent of my focus. I made a commitment to him, and I need to respect that now more than ever. I know I can't always leave my phone off, but I also know we're at a turning point.

For the first time in our relationship, we're experiencing something that's putting a strain on the ease we've always managed to have. In six years we've never gotten into a major fight, things have just been comfortable, easy. At first, I enjoyed the fact that we didn't have the overwhelming passion that I had with Landon, that passion was what landed me with a broken heart. Now I realize that I need to decide whether my relationship with Brendan is more than a safe escape. It feels terrible to think that way, he's my best friend, but for this to work we need to ignite the flame.

"Why don't we go away for a couple nights. There's a cute little inn not too far from here. We can go snowshoeing and just relax. I believe they offer couples spa treatments." Brendan smiles as I perk up at the suggestion.

We haven't gotten around to planning a vacation and getting away sounds perfect. We'll be busy enough that I hopefully won't be distracted by anything—or anyone— else. Having Landon back in my life has thrown me for a curveball. I thought I had everything figured out and that I was on a path I was happy with.

Now, I'm not so sure. I just need to figure out if it's because of the haze I'm in whenever I'm near Landon, or if this feeling is something that won't go away. Even before Landon reappeared in my life, I was searching for something, but now I need to know whether what I'm searching for is here or if I'm trying to make something work that isn't meant to.

"That sounds perfect. I'll pack for us while you call and book us a room." Grinning, I turn toward our bedroom as he dials.

Three hours later we're pulling up to a gorgeous little

inn. It's painted a dark green, which stands out against the starkness of the white snow. Smoke billows out of the chimney where a wood burning fireplace must be. The website states that they offer complimentary coffee and hot chocolate. It's been a long time since I've cozied up in front of a fire with a cup of hot chocolate.

It doesn't take long to check in and get settled into our room. I turn from freshening up in the bathroom to see Brendan lying on the bed, his smile suggestive.

Despite the beauty of the scenery through the glass French doors and the romantic feel of the room, I don't feel the urge to be intimate with Brendan. Shouldn't I want it more?

When his smile begins to fall as I just stand there instead of joining him right away, I push myself forward, returning with a smile that pulls his lips up once again. This time with him is all about seeing if we can rekindle what's missing in our relationship. Sometimes we need to put a little effort into lighting the fire.

His lips caress mine as soon as I'm on the bed, our kiss quickly deepening and progressing. He's doing everything right and my body is enjoying it, but something is still missing. It's this way every time we have sex and I don't know why. I've always put it out of my mind, but no matter how hard I try, it lingers.

Ignoring the doubt that seeps like poison into my mind, I put everything I have into being present with Brendan. I'm sure every couple goes through these dry spells, I just need to push through. The little voice in my head whispers that sex has never been strong in our relationship, Brendan getting more out of it than I do.

Shutting it out, I pull him down so I can kiss him. I take over, trying to show him, and myself, that we can make this work. That six years together has created something worth fighting for.

We move together, our bodies familiar with what the other needs until Brendan finds his release. Chewing on my lip, I hold him close, searching for the familiar comfort in the safety of his arms.

Smiling as he rolls away from me and props himself up on one arm, I brush a curl off his forehead. His hair is wild and makes me giggle.

"Why don't we order room service and spend all afternoon in bed." He wiggles his eyebrows.

"Oh, I was hoping we could go sit in front of the fire. That hot chocolate looked so tasty when we were checking in." My words are hopeful. This weekend is about us, but I don't want to spend it cooped up inside.

Brendan is much more of a homebody than I am, I like to get out and socialize. I've found that we've been doing less and less getting out as a couple, he usually tells me to go out and enjoy myself while he stays home, but if we're going to make this work we need to find a balance.

"That sounds nice. Maybe it's calmed down a little since we came in." He gets out of bed, tossing me my clothes before dressing.

"I'm sure we can find a spot." I grin, happy that we're going to explore.

He takes my hand and we head out. After we grab our drinks, we snag a loveseat right next to the fire. The smell of wood and smoke, combined with the crackling sounds as the wood burns creates the perfect setting.

As I look around, I appreciate how idyllic the inn is. If there is a place to rekindle romance, it's here.

As we sip our drinks, we fall into the usual pattern of talking about work. I try to think of other things to discuss, like we did last night, but we've been so stuck in our routine we've lost the experiences that create opportunities for reminiscing. My life lately has been in such turmoil that I can't think of anything else.

As Brendan talks about his goals for expanding his business, I listen intently. I hear every word and respond accordingly. During the entire time, seventy-five percent of my brain is trying to figure out how I feel. Talking with him feels good, like when I get to have girls' nights with Blake and Dawn. There should be more to our relationship than friendship. We rock at that part.

With a sinking feeling, I start to admit to myself that maybe it was never really there. After Landon ended things and my heart was broken, Brendan offered a safe choice. He's an amazing boyfriend, everything a girl could hope for, but the more I let myself really evaluate our relationship, the more I understand my heart never gave itself to Brendan the way it needs to.

This reality is one I'm not sure I'm ready to face, but it's something that's been getting louder and louder in my head.

The rounded toe of my snowshoe catches the snow, tipping me face first into the snow. Giggling, I roll over, brushing myself off. "Who knew this was so difficult?"

I'm sitting in the middle of the path, my feet tilted at an awkward angle as I try to figure out how to get up.

"I didn't realize you were so clumsy." Brendan's voice is teasing as he walks over and helps me up.

I'm completely awkward as I adjust myself and attempt to tackle him into a snowbank, but my feet get caught together again and I trip into his arms instead.

"I'm not used to having to maneuver around this much shoe." I can't stop laughing as I figure out my footing. I consider myself a fairly graceful person, I can walk in heels, I don't trip over random things—usually—and it's very rare that I fall down as much as I have in the last forty-five minutes. This entire endeavor has been hilarious.

Brendan holds me close, leaning down to kiss me. One thing about Landon reappearing in my life has done is make me spend time evaluating not only my relationship with Brendan since then, but also prior to. I think I was in denial about how much we needed to work on things. It's always been so easy, our friendship evolving into more was almost a natural progression.

Sometimes I wondered why there isn't more of a spark, that intense need for each other, but I put it down to the fact we were friends first so we skipped that stage. Now, I'm not so sure.

Brendan drops his arms, taking my hand as we continue along the path. The trail weaves through a huge garden that I bet would be beautiful in the summer. The snow adds its own magical quality that creates a gorgeous backdrop.

There is a couple having a photoshoot done, it looks like an engagement shoot. They're all over each other, obviously intensely in love. I wonder if they're going to get married here. It would be a perfect spot.

Frowning, I continue to watch them as we hike. They have a quality, a flare that just radiates off them. It makes me ask myself, why hasn't Brendan proposed to me? When we were in college it made sense. Yet, we both have good jobs, we own our home, there is nothing to stop us. So, what has prevented him from asking? And if he had asked, pre-Landon, would I have the same sense of excitement radiating off me that the couple posing together does?

Soon we pass by, and they're out of sight, but the vision of them together lingers. They look so happy, so in love. It fits. A weird feeling settles in my stomach. I want that. That passion.

We make our way through the rest of the trail, talking

about the funny dog that lives in the inn rather than the topic we really need to discuss. I know we're both avoiding it, I can feel a heaviness in Brendan's gaze as the day progresses. He's feeling it too, I just don't know where his thoughts are on the topic of us.

Once back at the main entrance, we kick the snow off the shoes and lean them back into the rack.

The rest of the day is spent getting couples spa treatments. It's not what I expect, I thought the romantic setting and relaxing experiences would lead to some sort of clarifying moment, but maybe I don't need clarity. Instead of talking about how we're both feeling, we spend the night cuddling and watching a movie.

It's intimate, and it feels good, like home. The idea of not having this comfort scares me. The idea of not seeing Brendan makes my chest ache.

The idea of settling into what's comfortable and ignoring the void, that makes me feel like I'm giving up the life I thought I would have.

chapter twelve

Allie

Parking my car, I take a deep breath and look at the bar where I'm meeting Dawn and Blake. My heart is hammering in my chest. I finally turned my phone on after three days. Three days of giving my all into my relationship with Brendan. Three days of not talking to Landon. Three days of really trying to figure out what I want and trying to come to a decision. The first people I contacted were Blake and Dawn. I need them.

Things with Brendan have been different since before Landon, but I never acknowledged how different until he was back in my life, that flutter making an appearance after being absent so long.

The past three days have been eye opening and emotionally challenging. I haven't been fair to Brendan for over a year. I've been taking him for granted and I haven't been working at things. So, I tried. A few days might not seem like long enough, but I woke up this morning and I knew what I had to do.

Now, I just need to talk it through with my two best friends—before I see Landon in a couple of hours. They always help me see things a little more clearly, calling me out on my blind spots.

Walking into the bar, I spot them in a secluded booth. They're talking in hushed tones and I can tell that they're arguing about something.

Both fall quiet as I come up to the table.

"Do I want to know?" I slide into the booth next to Blake and look between them. It's not unusual for them to bicker, their differing personalities often causing them to come head to head.

They have a silent conversation before turning to smile at me in unison. It would be creepy if I wasn't used to their weird mannerisms, even though they're behaving odder than usual.

"No, just silly sister stuff." Blake flags down the server.

"Uh huh." Narrowing my eyes, I look between them suspiciously.

We order, our drinks coming quickly as we catch up on our day. Once we're a couple of sips in, I wait for a lull in the conversation and finally voice the words that I've been trying to get comfortable with over the past twenty-four hours. They still hurt, still make me a little queasy, but in my heart, I know it's right.

"I'm going to break up with Brendan." Both of their mouths drop open, so I rush on before they can start asking questions. "This is a long time coming, I just didn't want to admit that more was wrong in our relationship than a weird dry spell. The past few days I turned my phone off, and I tried. Like really tried. I was present. I made more of an effort than I have in over a year."

Holding a finger up, I grab my drink and sip at it, trying to drown the constricted feeling starting in my throat. "We went away, spent two nights at a romantic inn. We played, joked, and just enjoyed each other's company. Something's missing, I think it's always been missing to an extent, but it's become glaringly obvious that we're never going to find it. And before you ask, yes, part of this has to do with Landon. No, nothing has happened. And no, I'm not breaking up with Brendan and jumping into something with Landon, I couldn't do that to either of them."

Dropping my head into my hands, I choke out, "I just can't pretend that what Brendan and I have is enough. It doesn't matter how much effort we put in, I don't think we will ever work in the long run, I just didn't want to admit it because I do love him. It's just not the right kind of love."

Pausing to take a breath and a drink of my margarita, I try to ignore the burning sensation behind my eyes while I wait for the onslaught of questions.

"Okay..." Blake starts, staring down at her drink as she tries to formulate her thoughts.

"Wow," Dawn breathes out, glancing at her sister.

"You know we support your decision, and if we're honest we're not really surprised. There was a spark that was lacking, right from the start, but you seemed happy so I thought maybe it was just because things were so intense with you and Landon. Have you figured out when?" Blake rolls her glass between her palms, unusually introspective.

"I don't know. This is new territory for me. Part of me wants to do it tonight, but then where do we go? Do I leave? Does he? Ending things with someone you've been with for six years, someone you own a home with, it's complicated. The idea of holding this in though, pretending that everything is fine, it's not fair to him. And I already feel like I haven't been fair to him." I choke up, my eyes filling with tears that start to spill over.

Clenching my hands, I close my eyes and breathe. I've held it together for days as I've come to this realization and I just can't anymore. Brendan has been such an important part of my life, someone I cherish, and I'm going to lose him. I just know that in the long run, we will lose more of ourselves if we continue to try to work at something that doesn't fit the way it needs to.

"It hurts to think of losing my best friend. I've been sad and angry, this mixed bag of emotions rolling through me. Mostly at myself for not listening to my gut when I initially said no to him, but then I wouldn't have the last six years and I realize we needed each other during that time. Now it's just run its course." My head is in my hands, my fingers pressing into my skull.

Opening my eyes, I look between Blake and Dawn. They're both holding back tears as they each take one of my hands. The blood rushes back in as I relax my fist and take hold of their strength.

We're all quiet as we think about the past six years. The thought of not being with Brendan scares me. What we have is safe, it's comfortable, but we both deserve more than that. In my heart, I think once he's had time to think about it, I believe he'll agree it's what's best. I just need to deal with the steps to get there.

"It sounds like you've thought this through." Blake's voice is understanding.

"How do you think Brendan will take it?" Dawn's question is cautious, her eyes on her drink.

"I really don't know," I whisper, my voice shaky.

It seems like time disappears until I need to leave to see Landon for our final physio appointment. I won't be telling him about my decision, Brendan deserves to know first. The only reason I talked to Blake and Dawn is because I needed to work through how to do this. There's no script, but I still needed to practice saying out loud that things with Brendan are done.

It hurts.

It hurts to know I'm giving up six years of loving someone, but the idea of letting things pan out into marriage and a family while knowing it's not what my heart wants, is more painful.

We both deserve better.

My nerves are shot by the time I walk into Landon's clinic and lock the door behind me. It's quiet, dark, and he's nowhere to be seen, so I take the time alone to hang up my stuff and calm the pounding of my heart.

Not talking to him was a challenge, but I needed to give Brendan my full attention without the distraction. Ever since Landon reappeared in my life, I've been trying harder in my relationship, but it stemmed from the guilt of talking to Landon, ignoring that it was wrong considering how he makes me feel. I needed to put that effort in without the guilt.

Maybe three days doesn't seem like enough time, but at the end of each night I had more clarity and I knew that even if Landon wasn't in my life now, things with Brendan would have eventually come to an end. And that's what I needed to figure out.

"Hey." Landon's voice startles me, I turn to see him coming out of his office. "Sorry. You were in your head a little. Everything okay?" His expression is concerned, his forehead lined with tiny creases as he examines the slight puffiness to my eyes.

"Yeah, just thinking. It's been a long day." I force a

smile, ignoring the way his eyes narrow at my attempt to fool him. I glance away, praying he doesn't pry. I've already been through the ringer today and I don't anticipate it will get better.

He motions for me to take a seat, his fingers working their way over my muscles. The pressure is perfect, soothing. There's barely a twinge of pain, which is a relief. Vehicles are easy to fix, bodies are not.

"Want to talk about it?" His eyes meet mine, the blue a little darker than usual. I can see the question he really wants to ask, but doesn't.

I shake my head. "No, but if you know any jokes I could use the laugh."

"What do you call a cow with no legs?" His response is immediate, a smirk quirking the corners of his lips up.

"I don't know. What?" I move my neck as he guides me through some stretches, waiting for the answer.

"Ground beef." The corners of his eyes crinkle as his smirk turns into a full-fledged grin.

Giggling, I shake my head. "A little morbid, but punny. Where did you hear that one?"

"They were telling 'dad jokes' on the radio all day today, I cannot claim any of these jokes as my own. I can keep going, if you like?"

He steps back, finished with the testing. When I nod, he taps his lips and looks up at the ceiling.

"What time did the man go to the dentist?"

"What time?"

"Tooth hurt-y."

He grins at me shamelessly as I laugh.

We work through all my exercises and he tells jokes the entire time until I'm laughing so hard, I can't do anything else. We're kneeling next to each other, smiling as he dives into another.

I'm cracking up so hard, I almost snort. "Oh god, these shouldn't be so funny."

Landon laughs with me, or maybe at me because I can't seem to stop. His eyes sparkle as he watches me clutch my stomach.

"Oh my God, just shut me up," I choke out around my giggles.

Before I know what's happening, his hand is wrapping around the back of my neck pulling me toward him as he whispers, "Okay."

His lips crush against mine, our tongues stroking each other as we moan. His free hand snakes around my waist, pulling me into him. I lose myself into his kiss, the way he takes control and gives me everything I've been craving. My entire body thrums with the force of emotions running through my body.

I run my hands through his hair, relishing in how right the strands feel between my fingers. Everything in me is lost in him, until my phone chimes from my coat. Brendan's text tone.

Yanking myself away, I close my eyes in shame. *What have I done?*

"Allie—" Landon's voice is rough, low, and it makes me want to kiss him all over again.

"I can't." Shoving to my feet, I stumble across the room and throw my coat on, tears burning as they beg to be released. Turning to Landon, I shake my head when he starts to speak. "Please, don't apologize. I just, I need to go. I'll text you later."

Before he has a chance to stop me, I'm out the door and in my car. I brush my fingers over my swollen, tingling lips.

There is no forgiving what I just did. Something I promised myself I wouldn't do to another person. I thought I had learned my lesson the last time, especially since I was the one who was left broken. I can't even blame Landon for it. I said those words knowing it would trigger him, because that's exactly how our first kiss happened.

Taking a deep breath, I open Brendan's text.

Brendan: I've been thinking about you all day. I wanted to talk to you about something when you get home.

My stomach feels sick as I drive away from Landon, knowing I need to talk to Brendan too, but I doubt what he has to say comes even close to what I need to tell him, because I need to be honest. After what just happened, I can't put off ending things.

chapter
thirteen

Allie

Pausing outside our door, I try to prepare myself for what I'm about to do, but there is no possible way I'm ready for this. I know I need to do it. I know he deserves someone who loves him and is tied to him in the way two people bound together should.

I take a deep breath, filling my lungs and holding the air until it hurts, before releasing it and opening the door.

I look up, Brendan is approaching me with a glass of wine and a hopeful smile. I start taking my coat off, his hands helping me, before he leans down to kiss my neck. I freeze, my heart cracking underneath the feelings of loss and guilt.

Turning, I look up at him and I know he sees it. He sees how red and puffy the skin around my eyes is. He sees the glassy sheen of unshed tears. And he sees the look of decision and sadness.

Opening my mouth, I freeze when Brendan starts backing away, his hands up, his head shaking. "No. No, no, no, no."

A tear falls down my cheek, his eyes tracking its glistening path until it stops at the corner of my mouth. Ignoring the wine, I follow him into the condo, reaching out to take his hand. The tiniest weight lifts when he lets me take it and I lead him to the couch.

We sit next to each other in silence, the words I need to say are heavy in the air. He knows exactly what's coming, I think a part of him even knew this morning. I couldn't bring myself to fake being happy when I knew I was going to do this eventually. I swallow the lump in my throat and wipe my tears away, only to have my vision blurred with more. Neither of us is ready for this, but it's necessary, for both of us.

"I can't do this anymore. Us, it's not working and it hasn't been for a while now." I choke out the words, watching as his face cracks and he starts to shake his head in denial.

"We can get through this." His voice is a whisper. "There isn't anything that we can't work through. That's all we need, we just need to put in the work."

Dropping my head into my hands, my head moving side to side as I voice the words I know will crush him, the words I promised myself I would never have to say. "I kissed Landon." My voice cracks, breaks as sobs wrack my body when I look up to meet his gaze head on. He deserves to have that. I won't hide from him. "I'm so sorry, it just happened, tonight. It's the first time we've crossed the line."

"Okay." His response isn't what I expected, neither is the monotone tone of voice. It carries no feeling, no surprise or anger. No emotion.

"I stopped it and left. Even if we hadn't kissed, I've felt for a while that things haven't been right between us, that something's missing. I just can't ignore it anymore. It's not fair to you, it's not fair to us, and it's not fair to me." Wringing my hands together, I try to maintain some level of composure, but my heart hurts.

Things with Brendan aren't working, but I still love him and the knowledge that I'm hurting him, it's the worst feeling.

He reaches for me and pulls me into his lap. I lean into his hand when he cups my cheek, closing my eyes as he brushes a tear away. "I've felt it too. I just didn't want to admit it."

I nod, unsurprised by his admission. There's no sense in pretending that things haven't been the best between us on the intimacy front. We've felt more like roommates with the occasional benefits than a real, head over heels couple.

"It doesn't mean I don't love you. We can work through this, we can find what's missing. Fix it." He slides his hands down my arms and grips my elbows as he pleads with me, unwilling to fully let go even knowing things aren't working.

We've been together for six years, neither of us can imagine not seeing each other every day, I know it would be easy to let the comfort and safety of our relationship keep us here.

"I love you too—I just—I don't think it's the right kind of love. And I think the past couple of years culminating in what happened tonight, it feels like we're forcing something to be more than what it is. You're my best friend, Brendan. I love you. But I think if you look deep into your heart, you know I'm right when I say that this feels like an inevitable conclusion." My voice is quiet, I can feel the strain in my face, the tension is making my entire body tremble. I look into his eyes, searching. "I think we're both so comfortable, the idea of starting over scares us and that's where the urge to make this into what it isn't comes from."

Grunting, he tilts his head back, his eyes squeezed shut as he fights the urge to cling to our comfort zone.

I bury my face into his neck, wrapping my arms around him. "I'm sorry."

"I'm sorry too." He holds me close, using each other so we don't fall apart. "How did we get here?" He sounds defeated, heartbroken.

I laugh through my tears before pulling back to wipe my eyes. "I don't know. I guess we both didn't want to admit that we're better as friends, that maybe we were trying for something that wasn't there. At least not for the long run."

Sighing, he tucks my hair behind my ear. He squeezes the back of his neck before eyeing me warily. "Landon?"

I shake my head, gnawing on my lower lip before releasing it to give him a small smile when he runs his thumb over it. "I need some time to just be me. I can't deny that the feelings are there. I won't lie about that, but I'm not going to jump from this to that. I feel like it would be disrespectful to what we had."

Sliding off his lap and I get up to grab both of our glasses of wine, settling in next to him. The knot in my chest loosens as we talk, figuring out what comes next. For the first time in over six years, we don't really know what tomorrow brings.

Linking my fingers through his, I squeeze. "We'll work through this together. If we're good at anything, it's helping each other through the tough times."

"Friends always, right?" He gives me a small smile.

I return it, a bit of the heaviness lifting from my chest as my eyes fill again, this time with a little bit of hope. "Always."

Landon

My phone rings shortly after eleven. I've been driving my brothers nuts with my pacing so their collective sighs of relief when they see Allie's name on the screen isn't a surprise.

Josh tosses me my phone. My thumb is shaking as I swipe to answer.

"Allie." Clearing my throat when her name comes out on a croak, I shut myself in my room and sit on the floor with PeeWee. He hasn't left my side since I walked in the door.

My heart starts pounding when I can hear Allie sniffling on the other end of the phone. In the background I also hear Brendan, it sounds like he's talking to someone. He's a little muffled, but his voice sounds off from the other times I've interacted with him.

I haven't been able to stop thinking about that kiss. It held so much power, the feeling of her lips on mine was so right, but the timing was terrible.

"Landon." Allie's voice is hoarse, barely a whisper. "Today has been—challenging. I know you want to talk about what happened earlier, but I need some time to figure things out and get a semblance of normal back into my life."

A crushing feeling washes over me as I tilt my head back to look at the ceiling. Kissing her was a mistake, one I knew she would regret, and yet I couldn't help myself. How could I put her in that position?

"Allie, I'm so—"

"Please, don't apologize for it. Please." The sound of

Brendan's voice fades and I hear the soft click of a door shutting. "It helped me realize a lot of things. Things I had already started to work out. I just need some time. Time to evaluate and time without distractions. I know it's hard to understand right now, but I need you to accept that I need a break to clear my head."

Tears prick at the back of my eyes. Knowing this is what Allie felt like seven years ago tears me apart and she's being much kinder than I was. "How long?"

"I can't give you that answer." Her voice is laced with pain and regret. I know she hates doing this over the phone, but I also know she's aware I probably wouldn't let her go if it was in person. I know because that was how I felt seven years ago.

"Whatever you need. I'm willing to do it. Just . . . promise me this isn't goodbye." I squeeze my eyes shut, just listening to the sound of her on the other end of the line. Holding my breath as I wait.

"It isn't, I promise." Her voice is whisper soft. "Goodnight, Landon."

She hangs up before I can respond. Pulling PeeWee into my arms, I hold him close as I try to prevent myself from calling her back.

What does this mean? Obviously she was at home with Brendan. Are they together? Did she tell him? Where does that leave my friendship with Allie? I hate this limbo I've been thrust into. I like to think of myself as a guy who has his shit together. At least I was until I crashed into Allie. She made me realize how much was missing from my life and how badly I want it back.

Now I've gone and potentially screwed my chances when I promised her we would be able to stay platonic.

Staring down at my cell, I wonder when I will get to hear her voice again.

chapter
fourteen

Mid-December

Landon

Locking up my clinic, I check my phone for missed notifications. An endless stream of texts from my brothers in our group chat, a few news updates, and several new work emails, despite the fact I shut down my computer less than thirty minutes ago. That's it.

It's been two weeks since Allie said she needed time to work through stuff. I wish I knew what that meant. This feeling of being in limbo is frustrating, and something I would never have tolerated in the past—but this is Allie.

The little man appears telling me it's safe to walk, so I cross the street and make my way into the pub to meet Kellan and Josh for a drink. They wave from a booth in the back, partially hidden by a pillar in the middle of the room. Smiling in gratitude when I see I have a cold drink waiting for me, I slide in next to Kellan and take a big gulp.

Josh and Kellan eye me as the big drink turns into downing the entire glass in one go.

They both raise their eyebrows, Josh chuckling, "Long day?"

"That's an understatement. My ten o'clock no showed. My eleven o'clock went off-roading, despite a severe back injury from rolling a quad, and then proceeded to bitch and complain about how much he hurt. My two o'clock wasn't wearing underwear with a very short skirt, she has a knee injury, so I got a flash of her vagina that looked like it should play a starring role in seventies porn with every exercise. My four o'clock sneezed in my face, while I was talking so it went right in my mouth. And my six o'clock had something for lunch that didn't agree with him, and he was an endless stream of gas." My tone is dry and I grow even more exhausted just repeating everything that happened today.

My brothers aren't bothering to hide their laughter as another beer is set in front of me. This one I intend to enjoy, but today was a clusterfuck of awful and that first one helped take the edge off just a little.

"You're the one that wanted to go to school for a stupidly long time to do a job where you have to touch people. This is what you get." Josh shrugs with a smirk, his lack of sympathy expected.

He co-owns an auto repair shop with his best friend and they have a woman hired specifically to deal with the customers so they don't have to.

Kellan can empathize a little more, he's a high school counselor, so while he doesn't get hands on he deals with the raging hormones of teenagers.

"It's a full moon out. At least that's what our admin

assistant told me when I came in this morning." Kellan grimaces. "I think it brings out the crazy in people. I had two girls who are usually best friends trying to pull each other's hair out today. And every teacher was talking about how off the handle their students were."

The smirk on Josh's face as we both wallow falls when he glances at the door.

"Shit." He shoots a look at me, concern etched onto his forehead.

Kellan and I glance over and the air rushes out of my lungs. Brendan is holding a chair out as Allie sits down. Doing the same for her friend Dawn.

They don't bother looking around the pub, and our booth is partially hidden from them anyway, giving me the ability to watch mostly unseen.

My chest aches as I watch Allie smile at Brendan as he takes the seat next to her, but they're seated about a foot apart. That's strange. I watch closely as the three of them chat. She looks happy, but I know Allie. I see the shadows under her eyes and the extra wideness to her grin which means she's forcing it.

I can feel both my brothers' eyes on me as I watch Dawn hand over some papers. Allie signs three pages and so does Brendan before passing them back and watching Dawn sign them too. She folds a copy, putting it in an envelope and passing it to Allie, before doing the same for Brendan. They look like formal documents, but for what?

Gripping the edge of my seat, I ignore Kellan's attempt to draw my attention away from them. I can't tear my eyes away from Allie.

I miss her and it's taking every bit of my willpower not to get up and go talk to her. Time seems to freeze and blur by all at the same time, until Allie gathers her purse and stands up. She hugs Dawn, says something to Brendan, and then she's out the door.

"Dude. You can stop staring like a lovestruck teenager." Josh shoves my beer toward me so I can take another drink.

"Is it normal for them not to show affection and then leave separately?" Kellan asks curiously. "Like they barely made eye contact and they were sitting so far apart, their friend could have almost fit between them."

"No. Brendan always came across as an affectionate guy the few times I met him." He always had a hand on a hip or a smile just for her. So, what's going on? I want to text Allie to find out, but I know I need to respect her need for distance.

We glance back over to where Brendan's still seated with Dawn. She's laughing at something he said and it doesn't look like they're planning on packing it in any time soon.

"That chick clearly has it bad for him." Kellan points out as she leans her elbows onto the table, her fingers in her hair.

Picking up my beer, I take a sip before returning my attention to the table across the bar. The wheels in my head are turning as I contemplate what could be happening in Allie's life. A spark of hope igniting as I glance back at Dawn and Brendan.

My brothers draw my attention back to the reason we're sitting here today. Kellan finally found a house and put in an offer. He moved in with us "temporarily" three years ago, but could never find what he wanted in his price range.

By the time he's shown us photos and told us his possession date, another hour has passed and the table across the room is now empty.

Glancing down at my phone when we're leaving the pub, I sigh when there are no messages from Allie.

"You're making me sick, man. She said she needed

time, so stop stalking your phone and go about your business. If you love her, trust her enough to come to you when she's worked through whatever it is she's dealing with. At that point you can figure your shit out." Josh elbows me in the ribs, rolling his eyes.

He's right. I know it. It's hard to reconcile the rational part of my brain with the emotional one that has decided to rear its ugly head.

When I get home, I snap on PeeWee's leash and head back out the door. He's been getting walked more than usual lately. It's a great distraction.

My gut tells me that Allie and Brendan aren't together anymore, but then why hasn't she contacted me? Maybe she's decided she doesn't want either of us. It hurts knowing that by kissing her, I may have not only ruined their relationship, but ours as well.

PeeWee sniffs along, oblivious to my inner turmoil. I wouldn't blame her if she wanted a clean slate. She has no reason to trust me with her heart.

Sighing, I turn to head back home. Allie said she wasn't saying goodbye. I just need to trust her, even if not knowing what's going on is driving me crazy.

chapter
fifteen

Allie

Brendan and I stand side by side in the empty space that used to be our home. It sold remarkably fast, which is a blessing. We packed up our life in three days. Today is moving day, it's heavy with the sadness of an end while also mixed with the tentative excitement of a new beginning.

"I can't believe we won't be coming home here anymore." I look over at Brendan, fresh tears filling my eyes. I feel like I've cried more in the last few weeks than I have in the five years prior. "I know it didn't work out, but I've loved these past six years with you. And I loved our home together."

Brendan wraps his arms around me, pulling me into a comforting hug. Possibly the last one I will ever receive from him. "I wouldn't change any of it."

"Neither would I." My voice is muffled by his shirt, but the words are true. I can't imagine not having these six years with him as my partner. We've grown so much together and going in different directions is scary for us both.

Brendan has been amazing to me in the weeks since that night. He's dealt with the selling of the condo—with Dawn's help. He's dealt with the lawyers for splitting the sale, and he came with me when Dawn was showing me condos close to work at his insistence so he could check some of the things I might not think of. He also had a buddy of his inspect it for free before I put in my offer.

My new home is freshly renovated and I got it below its appraised value because the owner is relocating for work. It was a steal of a deal, and Dawn was able to get me in there before the official listing was posted.

In return, I took care of all the packing because he hates it, ensuring everything was organized and labelled. Heavy with guilt, I'm positive no moving boxes have been more organized than the ones currently being delivered to his new home. As far as break ups go, I feel like we could go down in history for how amicable it has been.

We've spent nights reminiscing together. Our routine stayed the same, except Brendan slept on the hide-a-bed. There were tears shed, and we talked through any feelings that came up.

"Do you think there's anything we could have done differently?" Brendan sits on the opposite side of the couch from me, shadows heavy under his eyes.

That's the question I think we've both been struggling with, but there's no scenario that I can think of that changes this outcome. Even if Landon hadn't reappeared in my life, eventually we would've admitted that something is missing. I just wish I didn't have that kiss hanging over us.

Shaking my head I reply, "I don't think so. I've thought

about it over and over. Maybe if I didn't have the history I do. Maybe if we had met in a different situation, we might have been perfect for each other. I think it just wasn't meant to be, not in the way we both deserve." The weight of his sadness presses down on me.

"I guess I know that." He sighs. "I recognize that I felt something was missing too, it's just—I never expected us to end."

We sit in silence for a while.

"I'm mad that you kissed Landon. Maybe not as mad as I should be, but mad just the same," he bursts out. It's the first time he's brought it up, both of us not mentioning Landon for our own reasons.

"I'm mad at me too." The words are whispered, laced with pain.

Landon and I crossed a line we promised we wouldn't. It's something I need to reconcile before I talk to him again.

I haven't spoken with Landon since I told him I needed to figure things out. Brendan and I needed this time, I needed to show him that there was more to ending this than some other guy, regardless of who that guy is to me.

"Thank you, for everything. For staying you through all of this. In some ways it made it harder, you're still the man I love, but I'm glad we're not screaming and fighting. I'm glad we can part like this." I pull out of his arms and wipe my eyes.

"It's like we're grown ass adults who know how to communicate or something," he replies wryly, making me laugh.

We fall silent again, our gazes looking at the empty walls that once held so many of our memories.

"Is Dawn meeting you at your place?" My voice is hoarse, raw from the emotions I can't seem to keep contained.

He nods, smiling at me. "She's already there. I guess it wasn't clean enough."

Blake and Dawn have also been incredible during this time. We hired Dawn as our realtor, her and Brendan working tirelessly to find the right buyer for our place and the right homes for us. They both helped me pack and now they're each taking one of us and helping us get settled into our new places. It was important to me that neither of my friends felt they had to cut Brendan out of their lives, I think Dawn appreciated that since she and Brendan have always gotten along well.

"Why doesn't that surprise me?" I chuckle.

Taking a deep breath, we walk through the home we built together one last time. I grab Brendan's hand and squeeze it as we make sure nothing was left behind in the now empty rooms. Rooms that are full of memories.

Grabbing my purse, I pull the handle up on my suitcase and follow Brendan out into the hall where he locks the door one last time. The click is loud, final.

We look at each other in silence, no words able to express how we feel right now, before we walk away for the last time.

"Ready?" Brendan asks, his eyes carrying all his sorrow.

With a deep breath, I nod.

Once we're outside, Brendan opens the door to my car before clearing his throat. He holds the keys up. "I'll give these to Dawn."

"Thank you," I say softly, chewing on my lip.

We both start laughing at the same time.

"This is so weird." I shake my head, stepping in to him and giving him a quick hug. "I'm always around, okay?"

"I know."

I slide into my car, watching as he shuts the door behind me and steps up onto the curb. I wave goodbye, and head to my new home, my new reality.

The door is shut on the life I had. There's no turning back and it's a frightening and liberating feeling. An odd calm settles through me as I distance myself from my old home, my old life. A calm that tells me I made the right decision. It was one of the hardest decisions I've ever had to make, one of the hardest goodbyes I've ever had to say, but it feels—good.

My new condo is perfect. Dawn went above and beyond for me and Brendan. She sold our old place for exactly our asking price, which she high-balled. She found Brendan the perfect space with a home office that has built-in shelving and is separate from the rest of the home. That way he can arrange for clients to come to him instead of always going to them, something he's dreamed of for a long time.

And then there's my condo. It opens into a spacious living room with floor to ceiling windows. The balcony runs along the entire side of my suite with floor to ceiling windows to enjoy my view from if it's too cold for the balcony.

The kitchen is off to one side, a nice u-shape with a large bar. To the side of that is a large laundry room and half bath for guests. My bedroom area is isolated with a wide hallway. It has a walk-in closet and large master bath.

Every appliance is new. The countertops, cupboards, sinks, flooring, everything has been redone. And the paint is a gorgeous, muted sea green.

Setting my purse on the floor, I wander through the boxes mentally checking that everything is here and in its place.

Another way Dawn was my savior, she recommended

the top three moving companies and we found one that would move both Brendan and me at the same time, for a reduced cost.

I'm just cutting into the first box when Blake comes breezing in with a bottle of wine and two glasses.

"Take out is ordered and on its way. I figured we're going to need it, because I know you won't rest until everything is in its place." She smiles at me and I can't help but smile back. She has helped hold me together, her presence completely judgment free.

Blake is the more outgoing twin, her positive energy contagious and I need her to be her normal chatty self. That's why she's helping me. Brendan needs Dawn's quiet reassurance, which is why she's helping him.

None of his buddies were free this weekend to make the transition, which I think he was a little relieved by.

Taking the now full glass, I go to take a sip when Blake tsks at me.

"We need to make a toast first." She raises her glass and her eyebrows until I do the same. "To new spaces, new journeys, and listening to your heart even when it hurts."

She clinks her glass against mine and lifts the glass to her lips. The red she's chosen is bold and flavorful, somehow fitting with this new life I'm building.

"Let's get this party started." She grins, taking out her phone and portable dock. "I made a playlist just for tonight."

An upbeat song about new beginnings and following your heart blares out of the speaker, giving me an idea of the vibe Blake is going for. It makes me smile and appreciate the effort that she's gone through to make this transition a little easier on me.

We dive into the boxes of kitchen stuff. Blake unpacks while I wipe everything down and find their new spots.

The only thing I like about moving is organizing everything. I used to drive Brendan crazy with my penchant for rearranging furniture.

Brendan insisted I take everything from the kitchen, so I insisted he take the living room furniture. We both decided to get new bedroom furniture, needing a fresh start in there. Neither of us felt right bringing it along, knowing the memories we shared purchasing the furniture together—and christening it together. The idea of crawling into the same bed I shared with Brendan when I'm trying to get a fresh start didn't sit well with me. The rest of the belongings don't hold quite the same memories, and it's easier to look at a spoon and only see a spoon.

Brendan had chosen the living room furniture, it wasn't quite my taste, so splitting the household items the way we did worked for both of us. I spent way too much time shopping for a new couch set, but I found the perfect couch and loveseat in a weathered leather. Comfortable but easy to clean and the perfect size that if I want to move them to different spots in the room I can.

By the time our takeout arrives, the kitchen is unpacked and organized. There are so many cupboards, I actually have a couple empty ones and the countertop is so spacious that my coffee pot and toaster barely take up any real estate. Blake may joke around, but the music she's selected has kept us both pumped up and she's been an unpacking machine.

We take a breather and eat dinner picnic style on the living room floor, before tackling the bedroom, closet, and bath.

I finally kick Blake out after midnight with only the living room left to deal with. My new furniture isn't arriving until tomorrow afternoon, so I move the boxes to one wall and sit in the middle of the room with the lights off.

The moon is full, filling the room with light. The house is quiet, every new creak startling me. When the fridge turns on, I jump. Taking a deep breath, I exhale on a laugh, mentally scolding myself. I'm going to have to get used to being here alone, but a part of me feels the hole not having Brendan around has created.

My phone pings from the kitchen counter, its bright light contrasting with the natural glow of the moon.

Brendan: I can't sleep, every noise is so foreign.

Me: I was just glaring at my fridge because it scared me.

Brendan: I know we made the right choice, but it doesn't feel that way right now. I miss you.

Hugging my phone to my chest, I allow myself to feel the ache of sadness I've been ignoring all day. There were moments as I unpacked that made me want to turn to Brendan and ask if he remembered this or that, and he wasn't there.

Sighing, I shove to my feet, make sure everything is locked, and then head to my bedroom. Sitting on the foot of my new bed, I fall back onto my new blanket and write back.

Me: I miss you too. I had moments throughout the day when I started to turn to you and you weren't there. It was hard. This feels different than when we moved into our condo.

Brendan: I think we were too distracted christening every room to notice the noises. And I had the same thing, I would open a box and remember a story . . .

Me: Lol, I remember that. The next day at work I was exhausted and rocking the sexed-up look.

Brendan: I guess we should say goodnight and face the silence.

Me: I guess. Goodnight, Brendan.

Brendan: Goodnight, Allie.

Rolling off the bed, I plug my phone in and change into my pajamas. My bathroom echoes as I go through my nightly routine and I mentally add some decorations to my shopping list. It's a large room and it feels empty. Lonely. Half of the counter is empty, the second sink looking bare without anything surrounding it. Closing my eyes, I fight back tears. This is the right choice, but the hole feels big. With a deep breath, I open my eyes and spread my stuff out across the entire counter until it doesn't look like one half is waiting for its person.

Shutting off the lights, I stare out the window and look at my new view. It's beautiful, but foreign. Shivering, I finally crawl into bed and wrap myself into my new sheets, breathing in the smell of my laundry detergent. I'm exhausted and, despite the fact my bed feels empty, I fall asleep quickly.

I'm soaking in my huge tub, contemplating everything that's happened. If you would have asked me a year ago where I thought I'd be now, this wouldn't even crack the top one hundred scenarios.

My cell rings, interrupting my thoughts. Brendan's name flashes across the screen.

We've spoken periodically, out of loneliness and habit. It's usually quick, amicable, with an abrupt goodbye because we don't really know how to speak to each other anymore.

"Hey. Is everything okay?" I answer. Things have been quiet, and I know we both need to start giving each other some space.

"What does he have that I don't? Why him? Why not me?" His voice is sharp, laced with hurt and anger.

I breathe in deeply, my heart taking a beating by those questions and the sadness behind them. The worst part of all of this is the fact I hurt someone so close to me. That I caused someone to ask the same question that haunted me for so long.

The room blurs as my eyes fill with tears and I try to formulate an answer that he deserves.

"Nothing. He doesn't have anything you're missing. There was just a piece missing between you and me. I hate that you're asking the same question that plagued me. In another life, maybe we would have been perfect for each other, but not this one. I'm sorry, Brendan. I wish things were different. I want you to know that. I wish with my whole being that I could turn a switch and our relationship could be everything that both of us need. I just can't." I choke up as I talk. Hearing his voice, it makes me realize how much I miss him, his friendship and the aspects of our relationship that we excelled at.

"The end of us felt too easy. It was too smooth." His voice is thick, the way it gets when he's holding off tears.

I laugh, the sound harsh in my own head. "I've never cried so much in my life. Trust me, Brendan, nothing about this has been easy."

He takes a deep breath. "I guess I know that. I just miss you, Allie. I fucking miss you so much. You're my best friend and now there's a hole that's gaping and I don't know how to fill it."

"I miss you too." Tucking my legs up, I can't hold back the shiver that wracks my body despite the warm water. "I think we both kind of lost ourselves into our routine. We need to find out who we are as individuals again. Bren, you used to do so many things. We both did. When did that end? How do we pick it back up again? There is no easy answer, but all we can do is try."

"I know—I need to go, Allie. I just—I can't talk rationally with you right now, not like we used to. And I don't want to yell at you either." The phone clicks silent. I set my cell down and sink under the water, the never-ending ache in my chest flaring.

We both got so lost when we were together, I know I forgot how to be on my own. How to fill my time and not feel empty. It's something I've been working on.

Blake and I have started doing yoga together twice a week and I'm exploring other things I used to enjoy, see what will fit into this new life I'm creating.

chapter
sixteen

March

Tapping my fingers on the table, I contemplate the text message I just typed out. It's been so long since we've talked. Are my words too trivial? Should I even bother? Squeezing my eyes shut, I try to think how I would feel if our roles were reversed.

Sucking it up, I press send. The message is a simple "Happy Birthday."

It was excruciatingly painful having Brendan ask me why Landon over him, something I have experience torturing myself over. It's haunted me for months.

I haven't talked to him since the day he showed up at my door steaming mad before deflating and telling me he just needed time before he could look at me. That was in January.

Today is his birthday though and the idea of not acknowledging it is worse than him ignoring me or getting mad at me again.

Flipping my phone onto its face, I lift the lid to my laptop and start scrolling the cats available for adoption on a local rescues website. True to my word, I haven't talked to Landon since the breakup. I needed to give myself time to be just me. I also needed to show Brendan the breakup was due to more than my feelings for someone else. However, it's been a lonely several months.

Landon never strays far from my mind and I want to reach out to him, but I also don't want to hurt Brendan any more than I already have. I miss them both, but for very different reasons. In the past three months, I've never felt more alone or more torn in two. Torn between keeping Brendan from hurting more than I've already caused or reaching out to Landon and filling the gaping hole his absence has created.

Yet, if I'm being honest, I've learned so much about myself in the past several months. I took a writing class. I learned how to fix the toilet when it broke. And I started swimming every morning before work. As time has passed, my loneliness is there, but it's different. It's not out of a desperate need to be with someone, but now it's to find a person to compliment the life I've started to develop. That feeling is how I know I'm ready to pursue something with Landon, if he's still interested.

I scroll through photos of adorable cats, trying to find the right one. I've always wanted a cat, but Brendan is allergic so I could never adopt one. Now that I'm completely settled into my apartment and have established a new routine, I'm ready to open my home to one. I don't want to come home to an empty house anymore, so I can't wait to adopt a feline companion.

I'm looking for close to an hour when I finally find the one. He's a four-year-old black cat that's been with the rescue for three and a half years. His eyes are sad and my heart aches for him. Clicking on his photo to "learn more," I read through his profile and find my heart breaking even more.

He was thrown out of a vehicle in the middle of January when he was just a kitten. People saw it happen and tried to catch him, but he was too skittish so they called the animal rescue. They were able to catch him, but not before he lost the tips of his ears and tail to frostbite. That combined with some neurological damage from the impact, he's considered a special needs cat. Many people have come to meet him, but since he's standoffish and takes a long time to trust no one has wanted to bring him home.

He's the one, this cat that they've named Blade.

Clicking on the application, I fill out the extensive form. My fingers shake as I submit it, hoping that they feel I'm an appropriate home for him.

I pick up my phone when it pings, flipping it over and pausing when I see that Brendan has replied to my text message.

Brendan: Thanks, Allie.

He continues to type for several minutes, the little conversation bubble appearing and disappearing several times before another message pops up.

Brendan: I need to apologize for acting like an asshole. I was just missing you so much and lashed out because I knew you would let me. I know that breaking up was the right thing to do, but it took me a while to realize part of the void I was feeling was needing to rediscover myself. It took me a while to figure out what I want in my life.

A weight lifts off my shoulders as I read this. It didn't sit well having him be so angry with me. It's the last thing I wanted and the pain knowing I was the cause of him being so destroyed has made me feel slightly sick every day.

Me: I understand. It hasn't been easy for me, either. I went from living in the dorms to living with you, it's been lonely.

There's a lengthy pause before he starts typing again.

Brendan: I know I don't have the right to ask, but what about Landon?

Me: I still haven't talked to him.

Brendan: Oh. Why?

Me: Bren, we were together for six years, it didn't feel right. Besides, I've also needed this time to figure out who I am and who I want to be. If I'm being honest, it scared me to jump from something with you right to something with him. It would be like this cloud was hanging over anything that might have happened and I don't want that.

Brendan: Do you think he's waiting?

It's weird to be talking about this with Brendan, but I can't help but confide in him. After six years not having him as a sounding board has been a challenging adjustment. Not to mention his question is one that has crossed my mind. It's been four months since we've spoken, maybe he thinks I backed out on my promise and moved on.

Me: If he didn't then I guess we know it wouldn't have worked out.

We chat for a few minutes longer, moving to more trivial conversation before saying goodbye.

Several hours later, I'm sitting in the parking lot outside Landon's physical therapy practice. It's five minutes until he locks the doors and only his car is in the parking lot. Running my hands over my thighs, I turn my car off and grab my purse.

The beep of the lock makes me jump. Laughing at myself, I shake my head and take the fifteen steps to the front door. The bell chimes as I push it open, Landon's voice carrying out from his office.

"I'll be right with you."

The next minute drags as I sit down to wait, bolting upright when Landon comes out of his office, eyes scanning a piece of paper in his hand.

"I'm afraid we're closing right now, but I can book you—" His tone is professional as he continues to scan the document he's carrying. He looks up, pausing when he sees me standing in the entrance.

"Hey." My voice is soft. I can't help but scan his body, drinking in the sight of him. He looks so good, his hair tousled from running his fingers through it. God, I've missed him. Unlike when he ended things with me, this time I let myself think about him. Constantly.

"Hey." His voice is low and a little hoarse, eyes devouring me before he locks his gaze onto mine. "I was starting to think I would never hear from you again."

Taking a tentative step toward him, I lick my lips and clear my throat. It's taking everything I have not to leap into his arms. It's been awful not talking to him, leaving him in the dark, but I knew if I told him about the breakup I would've been more likely to give in to the temptation of reaching out.

"I know. I'm sorry." Taking another step toward him, I continue, "The night we kissed, I went home and ended things with Brendan." I try to keep my voice steady, calm, but inside I'm a quivering mess.

Landon inhales sharply, his blue eyes locked on me. We stare at each other and I know he's waiting for me to fill in some blanks.

"I needed the time because we had to sell our condo. I had to find a new place and move, and I needed to be on my own for a while. You tend to cloud my mind and I needed to show Brendan, and myself, that our breakup was for a myriad of reasons, not just because of how I feel about you."

Stepping forward again, I stop once there is a foot of space between us.

"I don't know if you're—"

"I am." He closes the distance, placing one hand on my hip and weaving the other into my hair.

He bends, brushing his lips against mine. Soft. Slow. Teasing.

Sliding my arms around his neck, I press my body into his and deepen the kiss. I can feel our hearts pounding in sync. Some of the same desperation from that night lingers, but this kiss holds the promise of more. The opportunity to rediscover what we had. My hands tremble where they run through his hair as he slowly pulls back.

My eyes flutter open, meeting his intense gaze.

"I'm sorry I took so long." My words are a whisper, my heart rampaging in my chest at finally being able to be with him in the way I've been dreaming of.

"Do you have plans for dinner?" His voice sends tremors down my spine, thick with want, but he pulls away and puts some distance between us.

Shaking my head, I watch as he goes through the process of closing before taking my hand and leading me out. He locks up, rests his hand on my lower back, and guides me to his car.

I watch him as he gets in the driver's seat and starts

navigating his way through traffic. He has dark circles under his eyes that I didn't notice at first, his face covered in rough stubble, longer than he normally keeps it.

"I can feel you watching me." His lips twitch as he glances over at me before redirecting his gaze back to the road and changing lanes.

Biting back a smile, I shrug. "I can't help it. It's nice being able to check you out without being flooded by guilt." Pausing, I try to find the right words to ask him about how weary he looks. I like the scruff, but the bags under his eyes worry me. "You look tired, still sexy, but tired."

He parks the car in front of a tiny burger joint before angling his body to look at me. "Work has been exhausting lately. I'm ready for a long overdue vacation."

He fills me in as we sit down, running his hand over his jaw as he goes over some of the interesting clientele he's been dealing with.

"I bet it makes you miss me, huh?" My grin falls when I see a hint of sadness flash through his eyes.

"I've missed you for different reasons than you being an easy client to deal with." His voice is gruff and I know part of the reason behind the shadows is the silence he endured from me.

Dropping my eyes to the scarred table top, I try to put myself in his shoes. Despite how painful and abrupt it was, he gave me a clean break. I left him in limbo and he patiently, or maybe not so patiently, waited for me to let him know what was happening.

"I know." My voice holds the burden of everything that's happened. This transition has been painful for everyone. I'm not sure how we could have managed it any differently, but I hate the weight of sadness he carries.

Before I can continue, the server comes to take our order. Landon doesn't take his eyes off me as he orders a loaded cheeseburger. Quickly scanning the menu, I pick a grilled chicken burger.

Reaching across the table, I link my fingers with his and hold his gaze. "I realize it wasn't exactly fair to leave you in limbo. I wasn't really thinking clearly, I just knew that I needed to have a clean break with Brendan. I guess in my weird logic I felt that telling you what was going on would've been too great a temptation."

"And did you? Did you have a clean break with Brendan?" His eyes are intense as he watches me.

Licking my lips, I nod once before shaking my head. "We're done and it will stay that way, but we've talked. Our breakup was cordial—until it wasn't. Today was cordial again. He asked about you, us, what was happening there. I told him the truth. Brendan was a part of me for six years, it's as clean as possible when you lived with someone . . . loved someone for that long." I try to maintain a neutral tone, but I know some of the sadness I feel over the end of my six-year relationship lingers in the words.

Landon breathes out a sigh. "I never thought about it that way. I've never loved someone other than you, even though I tried with Melissa. After I met you I realized that there was something missing there. I loved parts of her, of us, but it wasn't actual love."

"I know this is hard for you to hear, but I love Brendan. I'm just not in love with him. My feelings are stronger for you, we were in love." Leaning forward, I look at him, pleading for him to understand. "That being said, we can't jump in right where we left off."

Just thinking about how we did things last time makes me feel sick. I press on, my voice strong. "Our relationship started off on the wrong foot and even if you would have ended things with Melissa like you had planned, I think the weight of how we began would have crushed us at some point." I study him, his expression is serious, intent on what I'm saying. "We need to do this right this time. Take things slow. I want to get to know you again without the guilt of sneaking around. No secrets. No hiding. We need to fall in love all over again and this time do it with nothing holding us back."

His gaze pierces into me as he pushes up and leans across the table to brush his lips over mine. "I know. I don't want this to get screwed up again."

chapter
seventeen

Landon

Allie looks at me, confusion written across her face. The building we're standing outside of is a non-descript brick building that has seen better days. Some of the bricks have crumbled away, leaving holes in the walls, and there is someone sleeping in the stoop of a side door.

"Ummm, I know you wanted to surprise me, but this place is a little sketchy." Allie takes my hand, smiling at me as I lead her inside.

The door creaks open to a shadowy entrance. A staircase is immediately to the right and on the left is a long hallway with the lights flickering. It really is something out of a horror movie.

The scent of jasmine greets us as I lead Allie into the building. The further down the hall we go the more confused she gets, especially once we start to hear the music. It's faint at first but as we get closer to our destination it grows louder.

We finally enter the studio. Selena is dancing to the rhythmic music she has blaring in the background. Her shimmery belly dance costume flowing around her. The smooth sway of her hips is mesmerizing as she moves to the beat. Every step, every motion is graceful and smooth.

Allie and I watch her, speechless, until the song is over.

"Welcome! Please take off your shoes, grab a hip scarf, and we will begin." Selena smiles at us before finding a song on her iPod.

"Are we taking a lesson?" Allie's eyes are shining with excitement. "I've always wanted to try it but didn't have the nerve."

"Well then, let's try this out." I grin. I remember her saying she wanted to try it years ago, I'm glad it still appeals to her.

Selena goes over some beginner moves. Figure eights, hip shimmy's, and a bunch of other flowy moves that I love watching Allie master. She has a natural talent, her movements smooth and mesmerizing. Compared to her, I look like a robot, but I practice right along with her. I want this to be something we do together, not something I just watch her enjoy.

"It's official, I have no rhythm." I laugh at myself as I try to mimic the intricate footwork along with what we're supposed to be doing with our hips and arms.

Allie laughs, her hips and feet moving in unison while her arms arc in a graceful pattern. "If it's any consolation, there aren't that many male belly dancers so you're not the only one who struggles."

"That or they're not man enough to try it." I flex my biceps while making a face, drawing a laugh from her again as she shakes her head. She's always felt that it's sexier when men don't feel the need to flaunt their muscles.

"Oh God, that was super douchey." She rolls her eyes, following Selena's transition into the next move flawlessly.

Over the first half of the lesson, Selena focuses on teaching us the dance moves before moving into a basic routine. We have an absolute blast, Allie laughing as I try to remember the moves and the order in which we're supposed to do them. Selena grins as we tease each other, allowing us our fun while still teaching us.

By the time we finish, Allie is glowing with happiness.

"You're a natural." Selena takes the hip scarves we borrowed from her, folding them as she addresses Allie. "I have a beginner class every Tuesday at eight. It's full, but if you're interested there is a spot for you."

She hands Allie her card.

"Thank you, Selena. We had a great time."

Allie tucks the card away, looking longingly into the studio one last time before we head to the car.

Before I can open her door, she puts a hand on my chest and pushes me until my back hits the metal. My hands find her hips as she presses into me, lifting onto her toes to brush her lips against mine.

"That was so much fun! Thank you for such an incredible and thoughtful date." She tilts her chin up, her hand wrapping around my neck as she kisses me again. There is nothing soft about this kiss. I can feel her hand shaking as I deepen the kiss, taking control.

Until now, we haven't pushed for anything too physical. Allie wants to take things slow, which I respect, but this kiss holds the promise of what's to come. Every bit of need I feel for her is being channeled into the way my lips move against hers. The torture at being away from her for over seven long years escapes in the moans I can't control.

Our breathing is erratic when we part, Allie's lips wet

and swollen. Her pupils are blown as her chest heaves, her hands still wrapped around me.

I push away from the car when she steps back, opening her door for her. "Dinner?"

She nods, sliding into the passenger seat. Shutting the door, I adjust myself as I walk around the car. My head knows we need to wait, my body hasn't quite gotten the memo yet.

We settle on a quaint Greek restaurant, the low lighting and secluded booths perfect for a romantic dinner. After we order, I smile at Allie and lean in. This is our first official date and it's long overdue.

"I'm so glad we're finally doing this right." She tucks her hair behind her ear, smiling at me. There is nothing hanging over us this time, and the difference in her is palpable.

"I was just thinking the same thing." I smile back, but I can't help the influx of guilt that surges through me. I've never done right by Allie. When we first started seeing each other, it was stolen moments and sneaking around. Then I pushed her when she told me she didn't want to do the same thing to Brendan. This is my chance to make it right. Do things properly. The timing is finally lining up and I'll do whatever it takes to make her happy.

"So, I was thinking . . ." I wait, smiling as she pauses in folding the napkin into a swan. "You've always wanted to go zip-lining, now that spring's here and the snow is almost gone, we should plan a trip to the mountains. I found this amazi—" I stop when she flushes, her lips dropping into a frown. "What?"

She looks up at me and I'm stunned to see a sheen to her eyes. Her words are whispered, but they feel loud to me. "Brendan took me on our first date. It was our anniversary tradition."

The server comes at that moment to bring us our food.

Everything looks and smells delicious, but I'm still frozen, unable to appreciate the tasty looking dishes in front of us.

Allie looks up at me, her eyes betraying her worry that I'm upset. And I am, just at myself. It's another example of something I missed out on for making the wrong choice. Something I missed out on because of my naivety. The past is the past, and hindsight is always twenty-twenty. It's time to move forward. We have a ton of firsts ahead of us, it doesn't matter that her first time zip-lining wasn't with me.

"It makes sense that you would've gone. Who waits seven years to try something they want to do so badly?" I reach across the table and take her hand. "Maybe we could still go. I've never tried it, and I did find this amazing place in the mountains. You ride a gondola to the top of a peak and you zip-line down a series of lines until you're back at the chalet."

Her thumb runs over mine as her smile reaches her eyes. "I would love that."

We dig into our meal, the awkward moment gone as we talk about her new cat. Allie was approved to adopt a special needs cat from a local rescue.

"When are you allowed to pick him up?"

"He needs to go for a vet check, just to ensure they know he has a new owner and to refill his medication. I think that's two days from now, so in a few days." She beams at me, her excitement palpable.

"I don't have any clients that evening, if you want some company and help getting him settled into your place—" I leave the question hanging, not wanting to intrude.

Allie's smile is so bright, she lights up the room. "I would love that!"

"It's a date." I return her smile. It feels amazing to be able to plan these things and not worry about anything or anyone else.

We finally leave the restaurant when they tell us they're closing. We're the last two people, aside from staff.

On our way to Allie's house, I feel her glancing over at me. She met me in front of her building when I picked her up and I can see her debating whether or not to invite me in.

When I pull up outside the front doors to her new condo building, I put the car in park but leave it running.

Allie licks her lips, starts to say something, stops, and then says, "Do you want to come up?"

Nodding, I maneuver the car into a parking spot. Allie leads me inside. Her new building looks much nicer from the outside than her old one. It's sleek and modern with clean lines, glass balconies, and pewter accents.

The foyer is brightly lit, the tile floor so clean it shines. A guard greets Allie as we pass.

"Wow, Dawn outdid herself in finding you this place." I follow Allie onto the elevator, watching as she pushes seven.

"She really did. I got an incredible deal. The money I made from the sale of the old condo was a sizeable down payment. My mortgage is manageable, the building is new and safe, and it's close to work. All the features I wanted."

She unlocks her door, leading me into her home. It's so cozy, eclectic, and totally Allie. Her living room is a cool gray accented in jewel tones. Her walls are covered in black and white photos.

We don't explore the rest of her apartment, settling onto her couch with a glass of wine.

"I had fun tonight." Allie smiles at me, chewing her lower lip as she sets her glass down.

I don't have a chance to respond because Allie is

straddling me, her lips on my neck as she presses her body into mine.

"What happened to—" I groan out as she nips my earlobe.

Her lips crashing into mine cut me off, her tongue stroking mine as she winds her hands into my hair. My hands grip her hips before sliding up her back and under her shirt.

Allie rolls her hips into me, both of us groaning at the friction. The chemistry between us, the way we come together, has always been passionate and explosive.

Allie's shirt hits the floor, mine following shortly after.

She tears her bra off, leaning back as I suck a nipple into my mouth. I've missed the silky feel of her skin. I've missed how responsive she is to me. Every moan, whimper, whispered word is genuine. My brain is in a fog as we grope, grind, and devour each other.

Her breaths are coming in quick pants when I kiss my way back up to her lips. Her passionate response to me setting me on fire.

Pulling back with a groan, I cup her cheek in my hand. "If we don't stop we both know where this will go, and I know you want to take things slow."

She drops her forehead to my shoulder with a disappointed sigh. "You're right. I want you so badly, but we need to do this right this time around. I want to build a foundation to our relationship, not just teeter on a rickety platform."

Allie slides off my lap, handing me my shirt. We dress and she walks me to the door. She brushes her lips across mine.

"Goodnight, Landon." Her breathy voice makes walking out of the door challenging, but I know it's what's right.

chapter eighteen

Allie

The pen scratches across the paper as I sign my name one last time, the mound of paperwork and extensive contract detail out the expectations I'm agreeing to when I take Blade home. The primary ones that I agree to maintain his medication and regular vet checkups and that should the adoption not work out, I agree to return him to the rescue. It's one of the reasons I chose this particular rescue, because they strive to match the right animal with the right person. I try to still the shaking of my hand as I slide the stack over to the staff member.

"Take a seat while we get him ready." The lady smiles at me, I can't remember her name I'm too excited. Many of the volunteers came to say goodbye to Blade, their fondness for him moving.

Taking the seat next to Landon, I give him a shaky smile when he takes my hand before I turn to stare at the doors. I've been counting down to this day since I was told I was approved. I even put a countdown on my calendar.

His vet check went well. Blade has some minor neurological damage from when he was thrown out of a car as a kitten. Due to this, he doesn't move with the typical feline grace. He struggles with stairs and moving over anything that isn't flat ground. Aside from that, he's totally healthy.

Despite meeting Blade in several supervised visits, it almost feels like a first date. I want him to love his home, I want him to love me. Whenever I pictured my home, ever since I was a little girl, a cat was a part of that picture. And now it's becoming a reality.

The staff comes back out with the cat carrying case I bought, Blade's golden eyes peering out the mesh sides at me. My heart breaks a little when he gives a nervous meow.

I take the case, thank the staff, and follow Landon to his car. Sliding into the passenger seat, I carefully set Blade on my lap, cooing at him in a soothing tone when he continues to cry in his rough meow.

The drive to my condo feels like it takes forever, but Landon pulls up to the doors so I can head upstairs while he parks.

Yesterday I took a half day off work so I could get my apartment ready for him. I installed a kitty door into my storage room and built a special litter box with a lower edge to make it easier for him to get into.

Instead of the normal cat towers, I had one specially built for him with a ramp into a cozy bed, because despite his inability to jump he loves to perch up high and look around and I wanted to be sure he would be able to do so.

Sitting on the floor, I cross my legs and unzip the case.

I open it up and watch as he inches toward the edge of the case, his ebony head poking out cautiously.

"Welcome home, sweet boy." My voice is low, a soft coo.

When he inches out of the case even more, I reach my hand out slowly before running my fingers over his cheeks. He creeps closer, but then Landon comes in and he bolts back into his case.

Turning around, I smile as Landon frowns. "I'm sorry, buddy, I didn't mean to scare you."

In his hands, Landon is carrying a huge bag of cat toys. A variety of fake mice, some feather toys, and a scratching mat for him.

"Wow! You really spoiled him." The gesture is so touching, my throat cracks with emotion. He's been counting down with me, helping me get my condo set up to welcome Blade home. He even got me a collage picture frame that says "Fur Baby" so I can hang it up once I have my first photos with Blade. Then to add in this on top of that, it makes my heart skip a beat.

Landon sits next to me, kissing me before turning to look at Blade who's peeking his head out of the case again, his pupils dilated as he stares at the pile of toys Landon just poured onto the floor.

I don't know how long we sit and play with Blade as he gets more and more comfortable, but Landon stays the whole time. I fall for him a little more as he spends hours with me and Blade, not once getting bored or complaining.

"I think we should order takeout. I know you don't want to leave him, but I can hear your stomach growling." Landon laughs as I put my hands on my stomach and grimace.

"You're right, and you've been incredibly patient with me." I lean into Landon's side, my eyes never leaving

Blade as he continues to explore. "We've crawled after him into every room."

"It was a unique way to get a tour." He laughs.

I feel myself flush red as I bury my face into Landon's shoulder. "Oh my God. I only have one cat and I'm already a crazy cat lady."

I don't move when Landon kisses me on the crown of my head with a chuckle. He pulls out his phone. I glance at his screen to see he's ordering us a couple of pizzas. He stands, reaching down to help me to my feet before wrapping his arms around me. "Not crazy, you just finally have the finishing touch to your home. You've wanted a cat for as long as I've known you."

He pauses, tilting my chin back so we're looking at each other, his expression curious yet a little cautious. "Why didn't you and Brendan have a cat? It's all you talked about when you were dreaming of having your own place."

"Brendan was allergic and it seemed silly to not move forward with him just because I wouldn't be able to have a cat. It was a small sacrifice at the time."

Landon nods, giving me another kiss before dropping his arms. He wanders into my kitchen, grabbing us a couple glasses of water before sitting down on the couch. Blade has disappeared into one of the other rooms, when I start to follow Landon clears his throat. "He's fine, come sit with me. We can hunt him down later and force more cuddles on him."

Smiling, I sit next to Landon and lean into him. "Will you stay the night?" My voice quivers a bit, nervous to take this next step with him.

A part of me feels guilty that I'm so happy with Landon. The devil on my shoulder telling me I'm heartless for being able to move on so quickly after Brendan.

Then the other half of me has never felt so complete

and I know I need to accept things for what they are. There is something between Landon and I, something irreplaceable.

"I packed a bag and left it in the car. You know, just in case." He gives me that sexy smirk I love, the one that he gave me right before he kissed me the first time.

Even though we've been intimate before, being with him now feels like we're experiencing everything for the first time, maybe it's because for the first time we're just us without anything else standing in our way.

"Good. I don't want tonight to end. This day has been perfect and I'm so happy I got to share it with you." It's something I always imagined, us picking out a cat together and bringing it home. While it didn't quite happen that way, Landon is still here sharing this with me. It's a moment that will always just be ours.

Landon pulls my legs so they drape over his. Our fingers are linked together, I sigh as his thumb strokes soothing circles over my skin.

"When do you break ground on the park?" he asks.

"In May. The new contractor has been working overtime to speed up the process on her end, but you know how slow things move on our end, especially after all the incidents last year. The design is incredible and it'll be complete just in time for them to pour water onto the new skating area. It's a trail that will weave through the park, but in the winter, they're going to turn it into a skating trail. The plan is to have Christmas lights in the trees all along the path and hot chocolate stands at a few different checkpoints."

"That sounds incredible. We'll have to check it out." His voice is full of pride, his eyes light with interest.

Warmth floods through me as I nod. Ever since he's been back in my life I've been replaying scenes from seven years ago over and over in my head. Something I've just realized is that we never made plans outside of a few days and even then, that was rare. Most of the time we were flying by the seat of our pants.

Now when we talk about things we want to do, it includes plans for the future, things we want to see and do together, and that makes me want to squeal like a teenage girl.

Landon tilts my chin up, leaning down and kissing me. He takes his time, the sensuous movements of his lips against mine show me he is feeling the same way. When he wraps my hair around his hand, deepening the kiss, I slide my hands up his chest and wrap my arms around his neck.

Everything about this moment is unhurried. We savor the way each other tastes, enjoying getting to know what we like and dislike all over again.

Landon grabs my hips and pulls me onto his lap, I grind into him, his erection pressing into my core. I know taking things slow is a wise choice, but right now all I want to do is strip down and feel every part of him.

Running my hands through his hair, I pull gently and move my lips from his mouth and down his neck. I move my lips all over his exposed skin, the sound of his groans fueling me.

"God, I love the way you taste," I mumble against him before pressing my lips against his again.

Landon grabs my hips and stands up. Wrapping my legs around his waist, we don't stop kissing as he moves. I can't help the giggle that escapes as he bumps into the coffee table. He smiles against my lips before kissing me harder as he stumbles his way through my condo to my bedroom.

He sets me on my feet at the foot of my bed, pulling back to yank his shirt over his head. Before mine can join his on the floor, I glance at the bed and see Blade sleeping.

I put a ramp up to the bed so he would be able to sleep next to me if he wants to.

Landon follows my gaze. "Looks like he's settled right in."

Smiling softly, I turn back to Landon and press a kiss to his chest. Backing up, I sit on the bed, careful not to disturb Blade, and slide back, curling my finger at Landon.

"Come here." I chew on my lip, heat rushing into my cheeks at the throaty sound of my voice.

He smirks at me, crawling up the bed before lowering himself over me. I wrap my legs around him, pulling his head down to kiss me again.

"I love your lips. I love kissing you." *I love you.* The thought is so sudden, my lips freeze. It's not that I didn't think those feelings were still lingering in some part of me, I just didn't expect them to resurface so quickly.

Landon looks down at me when I stay frozen.

"Are you okay?" His expression is worried, I can see our past hanging over us like a ghost that haunts our present. I know a part of him is worried I'm not going to trust him and his feelings, but I do. I know this time will be different.

Nodding, I hug him close. "I just can't believe we're here. Life has a funny way of turning out, doesn't it?"

"Sometimes things are meant to be. Maybe not right away, but we just needed to live a little first." Landon leans down to kiss me again, his hips grinding into me when there is a loud knock on the door.

Landon huffs out a laugh. "Oh yeah, pizza." He kisses my forehead before jumping out of bed and throws his shirt on before rushing to the door.

Closing my eyes, I groan in frustration before rolling off the bed and making myself presentable. As much as I want to continue on the trajectory we were heading, I know it's for the best.

We eat dinner, talking about a pet playdate. PeeWee has never met a cat before, so it should be entertaining. By the time we finish, we're both exhausted so we head back to bed. This time we cuddle in close, Landon curling around me, kissing my cheek as he wraps me into his arms. "This feels right in a way I think was missing before." His tone is sleepy, but I can hear the smile in his voice.

"I know what you mean. I'm really happy, Landon." Closing my eyes, I smile at his agreeing hum.

We fall asleep wrapped in each other's arms. Our first night together. Landon doesn't push for more intimacy, something I'm both thankful for and frustrated by. It feels right to wait, to develop a relationship on more of a foundation than our physical attraction to each other, but the craving is there. That draw that we were never able to resist before pulling at me. I don't think I'll be able to wait much longer.

chapter
nineteen

Allie

The crowd screams in excitement as *Brothers Osborne* takes the stage. Landon's brother, Josh, won tickets but couldn't make it, so he gave them to Landon when he found out I'm a huge fan. I love this band and tried to get tickets, but they sold out before I had a chance, basically I owe Josh big time.

When the first song comes on, I scream with the rest of the crowd causing Landon to laugh at me. He's not a country music fan, but he knew how much I wanted to come tonight and he said he wanted to enjoy it with me.

I can feel him watching me as I sing along to the words. Turning to look at him, I return his grin and take his hand. Standing onto my toes, I kiss him quickly.

Song after song plays, until the band is leaving the

stage and the lights are coming back on. Landon and I have spent as much waking time together as possible over the past month, but aside from that one night he's always gone back to his house at the end of the day.

As he leads me to the car, his hand holding mine, I watch him. I want to fall asleep in his arms. But before that, I want to finally let myself be with him. I want to feel him moving inside of me, I want to see if we fit together as well as I remember.

"Stay the night." I angle my body to look at him as he drives me home. "I don't want this night to end, I want you to be the last thing I see before I fall asleep, and the first thing I see when I wake up."

Landon, looks at me before returning his focus to the road. "Would you judge me if I told you I have a bag in my trunk?" He laughs.

He smirks as I giggle and shake my head.

"Maybe a little, but obviously we both had the same thought." I take his hand and hold it for the rest of the drive.

Back at my condo, I pick up Blade and cuddle him to me. His rumbly purr is a soothing sound in the quiet of my home. Setting him on the floor, I feed him and then lock up.

Landon follows me through my condo, his hand resting on my lower back. Holding up a finger, I excuse myself to the bathroom where I take my birth control pill and chug a glass of water.

Taking a deep breath, I strip naked.

Landon is on the other side of the bathroom door. He's probably wearing his usual pajamas of sweats and no shirt. My heart pounds in my chest as I bounce on the balls of my feet. Shaking my hands at my sides, I close my eyes. This has always been the easy part for us, but our circumstances were so different back then. It's not wrong anymore. Maybe Landon will find me boring. I'm not a strictly missionary type of girl, but I'm no sex goddess either.

I summon up my confidence and open the door. Landon turns to me, his eyes widening when he sees me. He's wearing a pair of black sweats that hang low on his hips. His body is more toned now that he's older, that sexy V defined in a way it wasn't seven years ago.

Crossing the room, I press my body into him and slide my hands into his waistband to cup his ass. I tilt my head back and wait until he lowers his head down to mine, kissing me. He slides his tongue against mine, his intoxicating taste fueling me.

Shoving his pants down his legs, I wrap my hand around his cock and start pumping my fist. Licking my lips as precum glistens on the tip, I kneel down and wrap my lips around him. Swirling my tongue around the head of his cock, I look up and suck.

Landon's head drops back as I take him all the way to the back of my throat, cupping his balls in my hand as I swallow.

"Holy shit," Landon groans, his hands winding into my hair.

I devour him, loving the way he responds to me.

Pouting when he pulls his hips away from me, I giggle as he tosses me onto the bed and drops his pants the rest of the way.

I can't tear my eyes away from him as he picks up my right leg and kisses his way up my body stopping at the apex between my thighs. My heart pounds, my stomach full of butterflies, as he lifts my legs over his shoulders and teases my clit with his tongue as he slides a finger into my pussy. He works me over, remembering every single one of my buttons, until I'm panting.

Landon worships my body in a way I've never

experienced before. This time is completely different from all our previous ones. They were all hurried, an attempt at sneaking in moments whenever we could.

"Oh God." He presses one hand down on my stomach, holding me in place as he sucks on my clit and works his fingers until I'm clenching around his finger, an orgasm ripping through my body.

Landon kisses his way up past my stomach, my breasts, my neck until his lips meet mine in a passionate kiss. I can't tear my eyes away from his as he aligns his body with mine, the head of his dick pressing against me. He thrusts into me, my body clenching around him as I adjust to the intrusion. It's been months since I've had sex and he feels amazing, filling me until I'm quivering with need.

Our eyes are locked as he begins to move, slowly pulling out before thrusting back in hitting my sweet spot. He hums, a low rumble in his throat, as I wrap my legs around his waist and roll my hips.

His movements quicken as I start to clench around him. My body tingling as I can feel the release building until I fall. Landon drops his forehead to mine as his own orgasm follows.

Landon collapses next to me, kissing me as he wraps his arms around me.

"I've never stopped thinking about you or us and what we could have had. This feeling, being here with you, is incredible." His voice is raspy, full of desire.

His words should fill me with warmth, but instead doubt seeps in. The same doubt that I used to have when Landon continued to date Melissa even though he kept telling me he wanted us to be together. Its onset is sudden and paralyzing.

I can't handle going through losing him again. Being with him isn't just a fantasy to me, it feels right. But I don't know if it's one-sided.

"Landon, I need to know—is this, us, just fulfilling a fantasy? Are we an unrealistic expectation that we've clung to over the last seven years because it was something we couldn't have? I guess I just need to know that this is real. Looking back, I can't help but think about how you had all those chances to end things with Melissa, but there was always a reason not to. And now we're here, we're doing this, and I wonder if I'm going to meet your expectations or if the excitement is gone now that we're not sneaking around. There is nothing left to stand in our way and is the absence of obstacles going to take away the appeal?" The words spill out, ruining what should be our post-orgasmic bliss, but I can't help them. I need to know and I refuse to hold in my doubts like I did before.

He cups my cheek, his eyes flicking between mine. "Is this a fantasy? Yes, it is. I've dreamt of this moment even when I fought it, when I tried to create a life without you. The only difference is, right now it has transitioned into a reality. A reality I never thought I would get. I know you're scared, but I'm crazy about you and that's not going to disappear. I promise."

I stare at him, his words appeasing me a little. The worry won't go away immediately, but that's part of being in a relationship, taking that leap of faith and hoping it works out.

"Okay." I try to sound sure, but it's hard to shut the doubt out.

He pulls me closer until there is no space between us. "I know what that means in woman-speak," he chuckles ruefully, "but let's look at this as a new relationship instead of one we're revisiting. We're starting fresh and we need to build that trust."

Smiling, I lean in and give him a quick kiss. "You're right. We can't compare what we have now to before. We're older, wiser, and this is a real relationship."

He holds me close, the steady beat of his heart

comforting. I'm appeased, but only a little. We need the time. The foundation. It took a long time for things to feel steady with Brendan and me, it's going to take time with Landon too. I just hope that we meet each other's expectations.

Closing my eyes, I curl into Landon and kiss his chest. That's how we fall asleep, wrapped around each other.

chapter twenty

Landon

Over the next month I work hard to show Allie that the reality is just as good as the fantasy. We finally go zip-lining in the mountains, we walk every day through the park with PeeWee, and we end each day curled up on one of our couches with both of our pets, who surprisingly get along extremely well.

Glancing at my clock, I suppress a yawn when I realize I have one more client to get through before I get to go home to pick up PeeWee and head to Allie's for the night.

Shutting down my computer, I lock everything up and then head into the main clinic area. I smile when Carson walks in. He's a thirteen-year-old boy who injured his knee playing football.

"Carson, my man!" We bump fists as he comes in. "How's the knee?"

"It's getting better. Can I play again soon?" he asks in an eager voice.

"Let's check it out."

I check out his knee and then have him do a series of exercises. It's significantly better, but he shouldn't play quite yet.

"So, I have good news and bad news. Which do you want first?" I'm direct, but gentle as I sit down on the bench next to him.

"Bad news, obviously." Carson sighs, disappointment heavy in his tone.

"You can't play yet. However, you're close. If you do your exercises, I think you'll be ready for the field in a couple of weeks."

He nods, his face falling, but he works through the rest of our session like a trooper. At the end, his mom still hasn't come back to pick him up.

"Where's your mom?" I glance at the clock and see she's ten minutes late. It's unusual for her to be late, but I also know they've been struggling trying to coordinate all the appointments since his dad's out of town and she's managing five kids on her own.

Carson looks out the window, the crease in his brow smoothing. "There she is. She had to pick up Ty from soccer practice, it must've ran late."

He shoves the door open, waving as he heads out. "See you next week, Landon!"

Gathering my things, I race out the door while dialing Allie.

"Hey, babe! Where are you?" I can hear the smile in her voice and it's a soothing balm to a long day.

"I'm sorry, I just left work. Why don't you order Chinese, and I'll pick it up after I grab PeeWee."

Hanging up, I race home ignoring Josh as I grab my

bag and clip PeeWee's leash onto his collar. This entire day I've felt rushed and all I want is to get to Allie's where I will finally be able to unwind.

At the end of every day, whether the day is good or bad, the highlight is seeing her. She always manages to put a smile on my face and the couple of months that we've been together I've never been happier.

I'm still head over heels in love with her, but I think it's too soon to tell her. We need more time, we need to enjoy this togetherness without pushing things to move too fast. I want to savor our time, cherish each moment instead of rushing them. All our previous memories are tainted with hurry and secrets. Not this time.

Thirty minutes later we're walking into Allie's condo. PeeWee races off after I unclip his leash, searching for Blade.

Allie is nowhere to be seen, so I carry the Chinese food to the kitchen table and set everything out. I just finish setting the table when arms wrap around me from behind.

Turning in her embrace, I lean down and kiss her. I love being able to kiss her after a long day at work. "This, this is one of my favorite parts of the day. Nothing compares to your smile."

I wish when I was coming home to her, that this was our home. My head has moved into overdrive. Despite agreeing to start fresh, from scratch, my brain hasn't quite gotten the memo. Every time I see her, all I can do is imagine where we could be instead of where we are.

My brothers have moved from harassing me about crushing on someone in a relationship to harassing me about being so mushy. I just laugh right back at them because one day they'll be in my shoes. I love Allie and I'm not ashamed to show it.

"It's my favorite too. That, and having dinner with you

and talking about our day." She sits down at the kitchen table, breathing in the delicious aroma coming up from the spread on the table. "This smells amazing. I'm starving, my meeting ran long and I didn't get to eat lunch today."

We dig in, Allie telling me how the park is progressing. She's been so stressed out over it, but despite the strain and the immense weight on her shoulders, she loves what she does and her hard work is why this town is as beautiful as it is. She doesn't realize that she is imprinted all over, her touch creating beauty everywhere you look.

I had no idea until one of our evening walks just how much of an impact she's had around the community. Now whenever I drive through town, I get to enjoy it more knowing the woman I love has made it the place I love to live.

Every part of this town that I've always thought is perfect came from Allie. It makes total sense, she's had this hold on me from the moment I met her.

"I was thinking, we should get away this weekend. Take the critters with us and go camping or something. Blade has gotten better with his harness, I think he likes being able to go outside. You've been working so hard, you deserve a break." Pulling out the pamphlet, I show her the idyllic campground I found that's only two hours away.

There's a stunning lake with a hiking trail that goes around the entire circumference. Along the trail is a gorgeous, sandy beach that's secluded in a little cove, and since it's a ten mile walk from the campground it tends not to get to busy.

Allie flips through the pamphlet, checking out the photos. The campsites all need to be hiked to, and are surrounded by gorgeous trees and shrubs, giving complete privacy from the other campers.

It's perfect for a romantic weekend getaway.

"Landon, this place looks amazing. I'd love to go with you." She pauses, glancing back down at the pamphlet. "You know, with the park now underway, things should be settling down at work. I've banked up quite a bit of vacation time. Maybe we can go for a week, instead of just a weekend."

A smile spreads across my face. "You want to go on a week's vacation with me?"

She shrugs her shoulders and bites back a grin. "I mean, I guess that would be fun. You're all right."

"You're pretty 'all right' yourself." I smirk and wink at her.

We finish eating and then clear the table together. It's incredibly domestic, something I've never had before. Melissa and I never ate together. Even though she seemed determined to make things work with us, we hardly spent any time together. It falls on both of us, I was only invested in the relationship because of what I lost, and she was only invested in it because she liked the way we looked together.

That's what makes me appreciate every moment with Allie, even the seemingly mundane ones. They're what's been missing in my life. It's not the huge events that make a life, it's the compilation of the small moments, the moments that are often overlooked.

I don't want to take any moment with Allie for granted, you never know when they will be stolen from you.

The dishes washed and a fresh pot of coffee percolating, I fold Allie into my arms and kiss her softly, loving the way she fits right into me.

"Let me know when you can book your vacation days and I'll arrange everything else. In the meantime—" I bend down and throw her over my shoulder. She screams, her hands pressing into my lower back to push herself up a bit.

I stalk to her bedroom and gently toss her on the bed, my lips crashing against hers. Grinding into her, I groan as she deepens the kiss and wraps her legs around my waist.

Allie tips her chin back as I bury my face into her neck, kissing and licking my way down to her collarbone. She runs a hand through my hair, cupping the back of my neck.

Capturing her lips with mine again, I revel in the way she tastes. The softness of her lips against mine as we savor each other.

Allie sighs when her cell rings. Rolling off her, I smirk as she smooths her hair before answering. She sighs when she hears who is on the other line. Covering the mouthpiece she says, "Why don't we pick this up in the shower? I'll make this quick. I promise."

She walks out into the hallway, irritation heavy in her tone.

Instead of a shower, I turn the faucet on the tub. Once the temperature is perfect, I dig below her cabinets until I find her bath salts. Sprinkling them in, I check the temperature before putting the finishing touch and lighting candles.

Stripping down, I climb into the tub and wait for Allie. If you would have asked me a year ago where I'd be now, I never would have thought it would be here. Chewing on my lip, I find Brendan absorbing my thoughts as I hear Allie's voice muffled through the door.

He's the one topic we don't touch. I know Allie misses him, but she feels guilty about missing him because she feels like it's a betrayal to me. If I'm honest, I don't know how I feel. I know that she doesn't want to be with him, but a part of me doesn't know if they can transition into being strictly friends.

Sliding down, I sink under the water. I guess it's a non-issue, I doubt either of them are willing to deal with the discomfort of that situation—again—but I feel bad knowing that out of everything she's given up to be with me, she lost her best friend.

Sitting up, I run my hands through my hair and shake off these thoughts. Life is messy, and I believe Allie and I are prepared to handle the messy bits.

When the door creaks open, my mouth dries as I see Allie lean against the doorframe. Completely naked. She's stunning, her skin silky and smooth. Her curves flowing in a soft, feminine way that I can't get enough of.

Her hips sway enticingly as she crosses the room, her long legs teasing me as she climbs into the tub and straddles me.

"Now, where were we?" Her voice loses the edge it held earlier, lowering into a seductive tone.

She reaches into the water, fisting my cock. My eyes practically roll back in my head as she sinks down over me. Allie rides me, our lips locked. Every part of us is touching, my arms holding her close because I don't feel like we're close enough still.

Reaching down, I circle my thumb over her clit when I feel her begin to clench around me. She leans back, her hands on my shoulders as she rocks faster. Her breath quickens as her release rocks through her body. Her pussy grips me like a vice, ripping my own orgasm from me.

Allie drops her forehead to my shoulder, a breathy chuckle rushing from her lips. "We lost most of our water to the floor."

We both look over to where water covers the tile. Shrugging, Allie lifts from me and positions herself on the other side of the tub facing me, splashing me with a giggle.

We don't get out of the tub until the water is cold,

talking about anything and everything that comes to mind. We finally drain the tub, but when I try to clean up the mess on the floor, Allie grabs my hand and pulls me to her bed.

We crawl under the covers, lying on our sides facing each other.

"Tell me something I don't know. Something you don't share often." Her eyes are intense, the hazel more green than usual, and it feels like she sees everything.

At first, that feeling intimidates me, but then I realize I want her to see everything. I want her to know me like no other.

"Two years after I ended us, I looked you up. I couldn't get you out of my head, things with Melissa were awful, and I just wanted to see you. So, I went to the university and found you. You were sitting alone in the library, at your favorite corner table, and you were so beautiful and focused. It felt like I could breathe again. And then, before I could summon the courage to approach you, Brendan took the empty chair next to you. The way your eyes lit up, the brilliance of your smile, I couldn't take that away from you again. I went back home to Melissa and never told anyone, until now." My voice is sad, the weight of what I lost hit extra hard as I stood frozen watching them.

Recalling that day is painful. It was the first moment I saw what I could have had. Instead, I went home to Melissa. We were both so miserable but too stubborn to end things for our own reasons.

Anytime I contemplated ending things with Melissa, I thought about that moment and forced myself to stay.

"I can't believe you tried to see me." Her voice is barely above a whisper, her eyes soft. "It's been quite the journey, but I'm so glad we're here now."

Kissing her, I cup her cheek. "Me too. Sometimes things just have a way of working out."

She inches closer, resting her cheek against my chest. Her eyes close as I stroke her back in soft, rhythmic circles.

I catalogue this moment in my mind, it's the moment I realize that Allie still loves me despite everything. Opening my mouth, I start to say the words but I bite them back. I want to wait until our vacation.

chapter twenty-one

Glancing at my phone, I frown when I notice that Blake and Dawn are fifteen minutes late. Not unusual for Blake, but completely out of the ordinary for Dawn. Come to think of it, they both sounded off last night when I firmed up our plans.

With me moving and most of my time occupied with Landon or work, we haven't spent as much time together, neglecting our biweekly pedicure and dinner dates.

I know I need to leave the Landon fog I've been in, despite the bliss I've been experiencing with him. I've found it easier to ignore the guilt I have over how happy I am when I'm not around reminders of my life with Brendan.

Sadly, that has included Blake and Dawn. That's going

to change today.

I finally see them walking toward me, my smile falling when I see the glower on Blake's face as Dawn talks to her, gesturing wildly. Dawn is flushed, her expression worried as they both finally notice me.

What's going on?

"Hey!" I smile, cocking my head when the both turn forced grins in my direction. "Okay, I know I've been a little distant lately, but I hope you can forgive me." My tone is contrite.

"Aww, Allie, we know. We're not mad that you've been a little preoccupied over the last bit." Blake gives me a hug, and a real smile. "Trust me, I would have been disappointed if you didn't disappear into a sex-fueled frenzy after you've been pining for that man for so long. Besides, you had your grieving time. You did things in the right order."

I'm confused by the look she shoots in Dawn's direction.

"So—what's going on then." My voice is laced with curiosity and a little irritation. They've been acting weird now for a while and I feel like I'm in the middle without having any information.

Blake opens the door to the salon, exchanging another look with Dawn as we pass. "Don't worry about it. Sister stuff. I'll tell you about it after you come back from your vacation with Landon."

Turning, I give Dawn a hug while we wait for someone to greet us. She feels tense and when I pull away, I notice a glassy sheen to her eyes.

Before I can ask, she shakes it off and gives me a small smile. "How are things going with Landon?"

"Good, overall. It's hard not to have doubts, especially after the last time, but it feels right. I feel guilty though, like I'm happy too soon after things ended with Brendan.

And I also feel guilty because I miss him." I sigh, relieved to be able to talk about this with my two closest girlfriends.

"You do?" Dawn whispers, a weird edge to her voice.

"Well, yeah, not in *that* way, but he was my best friend. He knew basically everything about me and we spent nearly every day together for so many years. I think I feel it more because our friendship was the best part of our relationship and that's why we could part as well as we did, minus a few hiccups." Shrugging, I pause as a smiling woman finally comes to the front.

We follow her to the chairs, three foot baths ready to go with steaming water. As we get situated, I continue to watch my friends closely. Something weird is going on and I feel like I'm involved somehow.

"I need to ask. How is Brendan?" I look at Dawn, unable to resist voicing my curiosity.

"Why—what—how should I know?" Dawn stutters, drawing a sigh from Blake.

"Well, you've been hanging out—it seems reasonable that you would know. You've been friends for as long as he and I have been involved. Besides, I thought I saw you guys having coffee just the other day." I laugh, her reaction totally bizarre. "Dawn, if you feel weird that you've continued your friendship with him, don't. I would never expect you to pick sides. I think we're too mature for that kind of crap."

Blake snorts, but just shakes her head when I glance over at her.

"What?" My voice is confused, they're both acting so strange and I can't figure out why they won't tell me what's going on.

"Oh. Yeah. I guess I just feel bad because I don't want things to be awkward," Dawn whispers and it feels like her words have a double meaning. "He's doing well. I think he misses you too, in the same way."

"I'm glad. I want him to be happy."

We all start to relax as we're pampered, the pedicurist massaging my feet is pure bliss.

The rest of our day goes well, despite the tension between Blake and Dawn. It's not the first time they've had a major fight. I just can't ignore the feeling that this time their argument revolves around me.

When I arrive at Landon's house, I'm greeted with a note on the door telling me to come in. Smiling, I twist the knob and step inside quietly. The house smells amazing, something obviously cooking in the oven.

PeeWee runs to greet me, jumping all over, his tail wagging.

"Just in time." Landon rounds the corner, a single chocolate rose in his hand. "Dinner is almost ready."

Taking the rose, I lift up and kiss him, pouting when the oven timer goes off. I follow him into the kitchen, my stomach growling as the mouthwatering aroma hits me full on. "This smells amazing, what are you making?"

"It's a roast chicken, but a little more brothy than what you'd normally expect. I'm playing around with a house favorite." He grins at me, slipping some oven mitts over his hands and pulling out a casserole dish.

I take a seat as he sets the dish down, snagging his hand when he goes to move past me. Pulling, we smile against each other's lips before kissing each other in a slow, deep kiss.

I finally release him when my stomach growls again, taking the serving spoon he hands me and helping myself.

"How was your girls' day out?" He takes the spoon from me, but instead of serving himself, he holds my gaze as I respond.

"It was okay. Something is going on between those two,

it's making our outings a little tense. Blake is being super cryptic too. She was all, 'don't worry, I'll fill you in soon.' It puts a damper on our time together." I force a smile and shrug. "Oh well, I guess if they want to talk to me about it they will. It just feels like I'm stuck in some fight and I have no idea how to fix it."

Landon nods, his brow furrowing. "I can see how that might take the enjoyment out of your day."

I can tell he wants to offer advice, but he also knows that whatever advice he gives is no good if Blake and Dawn refuse to talk about what's going on.

Instead of dwelling, I dive into the delicious meal he's prepared as we bargain over who gets to pick the movie.

chapter
twenty-two

Allie

Straightening my dress, I slip my feet back into my stilettos, gather my purse, and shut off the lights in my office. Landon should be here to pick me up any moment now, and I'm tired of waiting inside.

No one else is in the building, even maintenance left half an hour ago, but I wanted to wrap up a few loose strings before we went on our weeks' vacation.

Taking a quick glance around, I shut off the lights, set the alarm, and head outside to wait.

One of the first projects I had was developing a circular park in front of the town office. There is a walking path that goes around the entire thing, leading pedestrians from the street to the main entrance of the building. At the north, south, east, and west points, there are paths leading to the center.

In each of the four pie-shaped sections, the mature foliage is a mixture of coniferous trees, lush shrubs, and thyme. All intended to be low maintenance and yet shield the center of the park from view.

Lining the paths are small solar lights that shine onto the walkway. At night, they allow you to see where you're walking without distracting or blocking the stars.

The center is my pride and joy of the entire setup. In between where the paths come to the center is a bench, but these benches are sheltered so even in the rain they are lovely to sit in, gazing out at the stars or watching the fountain in the very center of the park as the cool water flows.

The fountain is made of three stone pillars standing amidst black stones, the water bubbling from the top to flow down the pillars and over the stones. The sound of the water flowing is a soft, soothing sound, and I admit I love kicking off my shoes to walk over the smooth, wet stones.

This is where I find myself after waiting for Landon to arrive for over fifteen minutes, my shoes kicked off and tucked under one of the benches along with my purse, walking over the smooth wet stones.

The streets are quiet, so I close my eyes and listen to the sound of the water as I feel it run coolly over my feet. It was a long week of working late, but I feel the stress roll off my shoulders as I clear my head of anything but the water.

I love water, I love the way it sounds. I love how powerful it is in some cases, and how peaceful it is in others. It's one of the reasons I insisted we have a more interactive fountain. It was a selfish request that I knew other people would gain enjoyment from.

Heat warms my back, hands gripping my waist.

"Landon." I sigh with a smile.

A low, rough voice fills my veins with ice. "Nope."

A hand tangles in my hair, pulling hard when I try to turn around. The other gripping my arm in a vicelike hold.

"M-my purse is over there. Take it." My voice shakes, everything in front of me is hazy as my eyes fill with tears.

Instead of responding, he just laughs.

That laugh sends my already racing heart into overdrive and I start begging and struggling to pull away. He yanks on my hair, sharp pains shooting through my scalp. When I cry out in agony, he yanks even harder.

"Shut the fuck up, bitch." He drags me backwards to one of the benches. The previous serenity I found in the seclusion of what I thought of as my Zen garden, is shattered as he shoves me face first into the wood.

Sobbing, I clench my hands into fists. Where is Landon? Why isn't he here yet?

My flight instinct kicks into high gear when I feel my attacker's hand slid up my dress. I start struggling, kicking back at him. When he yelps as I make contact, my moment of satisfaction is fleeting. A blow hits me in the back of my head, a second one quickly following when I cry out.

Tears flow down my cheeks as his hand finds its way up my dress and onto my ass. My body shivers in repulsion as he squeezes and presses his jean-clad erection into me.

"God, yes," he groans, the sound fills me with rage.

I try to throw myself away from him, fists and feet flying, but his hand in my hair tightens and uses my momentum to throw me face first onto the ground.

My vision grows fuzzy as he pulls my head up and boots me in the ribs. Crying out in pain, I sob as my limbs grow weak. In his rage, he continues to beat me until I'm a puddle on the ground.

I can't stop one final wail from escaping as I feel him straddle my legs, my dress bunching up at my waist.

One final blow to the back of my head, and my world goes black.

chapter twenty-three

Landon

Glancing at the clock, I hold back a sigh of frustration. My client was thirty minutes late, and now she's telling me she doesn't fully understand the exercises I've given her.

Running through them again, I watch, giving minor corrections along the way. By the time we're done, I'm running close to forty-five minutes behind.

"May I use your bathroom before I go?" She dances in the spot, her grin wide.

Clenching my jaw, I jerk my head in a nod. I'm not disguising my irritation well, but she's been incredibly inconsiderate. She's lucky I didn't have any clients after her.

Rushing around the clinic, I check all the doors and shut my computer down. I contemplate texting Allie, but she mentioned working until I got to her office, so I decide against it. I know she has a checklist of things to get done, I don't want to bother her.

I finally hear the toilet flush—once, and then again.

Gloria comes shuffling out, her face bright red. "So, uh, the toilet wouldn't flush and now water is running over." Her voice is humiliated, and I have to fight to keep my expression neutral. "I'm sorry."

"Don't worry about it." I lock up after she leaves, almost positive she will be looking up a new physical therapist before coming back here.

Racing into the bathroom, I take one quick glance at the mess and yell, "Shit!"

Water is overflowing, the plunger askew in the toilet. I don't even want to think about what I'm walking in as I rush to the toilet and turn off the water.

This evening is not going how I planned. I was supposed to be with Allie right now. Hugging her and loving on her. Not ankle deep in toilet water.

"Why can't people show up on time?" Grumbling, I work the plunger until the tell-tale gurgle of a cleared pipe sounds. Turning the water back on, I watch it fill to the appropriate level and stop.

I make quick work of cleaning up the mess, unwilling to leave it for the cleaning staff. I'm not a complete ass, it wouldn't be fair to them.

I'm really running late by the time I lock up, late enough that I stop for flowers to soften Allie. Our bags are in my car, but I have a feeling we may need to delay our vacation until tomorrow.

Parking out front, I frown when I notice the lights are out and Allie is nowhere to be seen. Maybe she went home, but she didn't text. I'm not sure why she would leave, but maybe she forgot to pack something.

An uneasy feeling settles into my gut. Allie is great at

communicating, so the fact that I haven't heard from her and she's nowhere to be seen isn't sitting well.

I pick up my phone and call Allie. Straight to voicemail. The churning in my stomach increases as I head to her house, only to find she's not there either.

I search for Allie, unable to call anyone who might know where she is because I don't have their contact information. I'm about to head to the police when the phone rings with a number I never thought would ever call me again.

chapter twenty-four

Beep. Beep. Beep.

Beep. Beep. Beep.

Beep. Beep. Beep.

Blinking, I try to check out my surroundings, the noises and smells unfamiliar, but everything is out of focus. My eyes are so dry, they burn, and my head starts pounding at the bright lights. The constant beeping matches the throbbing in my head.

Groaning, I lick my dry lips and try to roll to my side, squeezing my eyes shut.

"Owww." The cry escapes from my lips almost like it's being torn out.

My entire body hurts.

Where am I?

Clenching my eyes, I try to ground myself before opening my eyes once again. Squinting, I slowly focus on the stark white room around me. As I take in the tell-tale hospital equipment, memories of what happened come flooding to the surface.

The absolute disgust at feeling that vile man's erection pressing into me makes bile rise in my throat. I lean over the edge of the bed, grasping for the garbage can and lifting it just in time.

My heart rate spikes as I think about all the possibilities of what he could have done to me after he knocked me out and a nurse comes bustling into the room.

"Shhh, you're okay, honey. I'm going to turn up the morphine and go find the doctor. Just relax, you're safe." Her voice is soothing as she fiddles with the IV next to me. Her hair is a mess of curls swaying in a ponytail, her expression concerned as I look at her silently from blurry eyes.

The pain ebbs as the drip takes effect, but I can't stop the tears from flowing down my cheeks. The physical pain may be gone, but emotionally I feel beaten to a pulp. It's hard to articulate exactly how I'm feeling right now, all I know is that my life will never be the same.

"What time is it?" My voice is hoarse, I must have been screaming when he knocked me out.

"It's eleven in the evening. You were brought here by ambulance at around eight forty-five."

My heart sinks. I have no idea what time he knocked me out at and my mind automatically goes to the worst-case scenario. I never thought something like that would happen in this town. I've always felt so safe here. My world has been shattered and I don't even know how to begin to deal with the influx of thoughts flooding me right now.

The idea of leaving this room, going back out into the world, is overwhelming and terrifying.

Crying out as sobs wrack my body, I fist the sheets in my hands and try to fight off the panic. Squeezing my eyes shut, questions flood my mind. How did I get here? Did he finish what he set out to do?

Is he still out there?

A masculine voice breaks through my thoughts, strong fingers probing my ribs. I can't hear anything he is saying over the rush of panic.

Screams fill the room and it's not until that soothing voice belonging to the sweet nurse breaks through that I realize they're coming from me.

"Shhh, honey, this is Doctor Anders. He's here to talk to you." Her cool hand smooths over my forehead before she takes my hand and squeezes it gently.

Opening my eyes, I meet her kind gaze. Her warm brown eyes smiling down at me in concern. "We know you've been through something traumatic, but you're safe now. You're safe."

She repeats that I'm safe several times until my eyes clear and my heart rate drops, and then she steps aside so I can meet the gray gaze of the doctor. He's got to be in his sixties, his graying hair trimmed neatly. The smile he turns on is warm and instantly puts me at ease.

"Miss Vincent, I'm Doctor Anders. Before we dive into your injuries, I want to let you know that we completed a rape kit, and the results came back negative. As you were unconscious, we gained permission from your emergency contact that we had on file. It was stipulated he could give medical permission to treatment should you be unable. The police were called, and they will want to talk to you at some point." He pauses and grabs my chart from where he set it on my food tray. "Now, I'm sure you're feeling quite a bit of pain. You have four fractured ribs, a minor concussion, and several contusions over your body."

His voice drowns out as I relive what happened to me. I know I should be paying attention to what he's saying, but all I can hear is that horrible voice taunting in my head.

I sit there, feigning attention, my eyes on the doctor, but replaying each moment. Never once in my life did I think I would be the victim of an attempted rape. I was supposed to be in Landon's car with him, on our way to go camping. Our town is supposed to be safe. I've never heard of anyone being attacked while out. It never crossed my mind to think twice about waiting outside for Landon.

Dr. Anders wraps up his instructions, checks my ribs and my pupils, and leaves the room. The rhythmic beeping of the machinery is the only sound in the room. Glancing around, I spot my purse sitting on a chair pulled up next to my bed. I find my phone, sighing when I discover the battery is dead.

There is a light tap on the door before it inches open, Brendan's head peeking in. His brow is creased, his hair all over the place. His eyes are bloodshot, almost like he's been crying or rubbing them. "Oh my God, Allie. When the hospital called me I almost had a heart attack. You never updated your emergency contact, so I called your parents. They're on their way home, they said they'll be a few days."

He comes in the room, Dawn following close behind.

It seems trivial considering what happened, but the first thing I notice is the fact that they're holding hands. My eyes dart to Dawn and back down to see her pulling her hand away.

She avoids my gaze when I look back up. All of a sudden her weird behavior makes perfect sense. I know Dawn, she's flooded with guilt, but she shouldn't be.

Brendan and I aren't together, and I've known for a long time that she likes Brendan as more than a friend. It makes me happy to see them happy.

"What did the doctor say?" Dawn's calm, low voice is soothing, and as much as I love Blake, I'm glad that Dawn is here and not her. She would be bustling around the room, her energy all over the place.

"Ummm, if I'm being honest I kind of tuned him out." I feel my cheeks flush as they gape at me. Squirming under their scrutiny, I lash out, "I figure I have a good reason to be a little out of it. I was almost raped."

Dawn's eyes fill with tears, trembling fingers covering her lips. I instantly feel guilty. It's not their fault that they want the information and I know I should have listened. This whole situation is overwhelming and all I want is Landon and I can't even get ahold of him. He's undoubtedly so worried.

"I'm sorry, that wasn't nice. I'm just tired and scared, and my phone is dead so I can't even contact Landon and he's got to be so worried." I start to cry.

The bed dips as Brendan sits next to me, his arms pulling me into his chest as he hushes me down. Dawn sits on the other side of the bed, rubbing my back.

"I have my charger in the car, I'll get it so you can charge your phone. Until then, I can call Landon." Brendan gives me one last squeeze. "I still have his number from when I called about your party. I'll be right back."

He disappears into the hall, the door shutting behind him.

I lean into Dawn, feeling better knowing that soon Landon will be here. I can't imagine the panic he's in. I don't say anything as we wait, but I can feel Dawn growing restless.

"Allie, this isn't how I wanted you to find out . . ." Dawn

starts, her voice filled with remorse.

Taking her hand, I smile. "You both look happy, so I'm happy. You two make sense. Let's not worry about anything else."

Wincing as she hugs me, I hold back a whimper because we both need the comfort of being held together.

chapter
twenty-five

Landon

"Hello?" I can hear the panic in my voice. I don't recognize the number, but at this point I will answer anyone who calls if there is the chance they know where Allie is.

"Hey, Landon. It's Brendan. I'm at the hospital. Allie was attacked this evening. They called me because I was still listed as her emergency contact from when we came here a couple of years ago. Her phone's dead, which is why she hasn't called, but I know she wants you here." His words come out in a rush, so fast I barely have time to process before he's done.

He runs through the details, but there isn't much he can tell me because Allie didn't know much. My heart pounds so hard it feels like it's going to burst out of my chest.

"Thank you for calling me. I know this is awkward, but

if you can tell her I'll be there as soon as possible, I would really appreciate it." I'm already pulling an illegal u-turn, praying I don't get pulled over. It feels weird to be getting this info from Brendan, but he's being surprisingly nice about it. He could easily have ignored the fact I'm not there, he could have ignored the call from the hospital, but he didn't.

"She's going to be okay, Landon." His voice is reassuring, confident. "It'll take some time, and knowing Allie her world has been rocked on its axis—she's always been somewhat of an idealist—but I know you'll be able to help her through this."

"Thanks, Brendan." I hang up and press on the gas, speeding as much as I can without drawing attention. The need to get to her is so intense, I'm in pain. I won't feel better until I'm holding her in my arms.

I arrive to the hospital in under twenty minutes, parking and racing inside. I don't care if I get a parking ticket, I'm not wasting time grabbing a pass.

I race through the maze of hallways, because why would a hospital be easy to navigate?

"Is she okay?" I finally see Brendan and Dawn, the surprise at seeing her sitting on his lap diminished by the desperate need to see for myself that Allie is okay.

A nurse comes out of her room, leaving the door open a crack. "You have an hour before we need to ask you to leave. We've extended Allie's visiting hours due to the circumstances of her being here." She gives us all a pointed look before heading back to the nurses' station.

"We're going to head out. Allie has my cell charger, let her know we can pick it up tomorrow." Brendan gives me a small smile as he takes Dawn's hand.

Nodding, I don't give them a second glance as I head into her room.

Shutting the door behind me, I can't tear my eyes off Allie. I feel sick to my stomach when I see the scrapes on her face and the defeated look in her eyes.

The guilt I feel is making me sick. If I wasn't so late she wouldn't have been in that park and this wouldn't have happened to her.

"I'm so sorry, Allie." Sitting on the bed, I take her hand and run my thumb over her knuckles, biting back tears when I flip her hand over and see the bruising on her palm. There are little dents where pebbles dug into her palm.

She closes her eyes, swallowing hard. When she meets my gaze again, tears have filled her eyes and her lips are quivering. "Where were you? Why didn't you call?" Her voice is tired, angry, hurt. A myriad of emotions letting me know I've disappointed her.

It makes sense that she would ask that. I was just thinking the same thing, but it hurts that those are the first words out of her mouth. I let her down in the worst kind of way.

"My appointment ran long, and then I had a plumbing issue at the clinic. I should have called. I'm so sorry I didn't." I reach out to tuck a hair behind her ear, freezing when she flinches. "Allie, I'm never going to hurt you." My voice is low, earnest, holding a tinge of pain.

"I know that." She licks her lips, wiping at her eyes.

"Do you? Because I reached out to tuck hair behind your ear and you flinched." I drop my hand to my lap.

"Landon, it's going to take me a while to get over this. I was almost raped. I have four fractured ribs and a mild concussion. And my body is bruised from head to toe," she snaps at me, pulling her hand away and crossing her arms. The move is so defensive, it cuts deep that she feels the need to protect herself from even me.

Then her words sink in.

"Brendan said you were attacked." I force the next words out. "Not that you were almost raped." I can feel the blood drain from my face, the reality of the situation sinking in.

She drops her arms from their defensive position. Reaching out, she grabs my arm and pulls me down to lay next to her.

"I think we need to not think about it right now. I just want you to hold me, I feel like I'm about to fall apart." She tucks her face into my chest, her body trembling. "I don't want to fight with you."

I hug her to me, holding her to me as tight as I can without hurting her. "I don't know why words are coming out wrong. The thought of you being hurt makes me crazy."

"I was so scared, Landon. It's obvious he's done this before, there was a method to how he intentionally kept my face pinned and in a way so I couldn't see him." She shudders, burrowing into me more, wincing. "I can still *feel* him against me."

We hold on to each other. I know the physical wounds will heal, but I look into her eyes and I see the emotional and mental toll she's struggling with. Her work is no longer a safe place, her town is no longer a safe place, and how does she get past that?

Rage fills me as I think about the person that did this to her. It boggles my mind that anyone could possibly think that's okay. What's even worse is that he's still out there, stalking his next prey.

The room is quiet except for the sounds of the medical machinery. Allie's arms are tight around me, it's like she's trying to soak up my warmth. She doesn't know it, but she's holding me together just as much as I'm holding her together.

She tucks her head under my chin, cuddling up as close as possible.

"Please don't leave me," she sighs out.

"I won't," I promise.

Her breathing grows deeper, evening out as she falls asleep in my arms.

✳ ✳ ✳

Allie

I wake up, groggy as I tune in to Landon having a heated argument with my nurse.

"I don't care about hospital policy. She asked me not to leave her, so I'm staying. Unless you want to wake her up and explain to her that she needs to spend the night alone after being attacked." Landon's arms are still around me, his muscles flexing as he hisses at her.

"Sir, unless you're listed as family or her spouse I can't do anything about it." The nurse is firm.

Prying my eyes open, I glance at the clock and groan when I realize I've only been asleep for an hour.

"Please let him stay. I need him." My voice is hoarse, my throat on fire.

Groaning, I roll over and attempt to sit up.

Landon practically growls at the poor nurse as I shift on the bed, the lines of fluid swinging as I try not to get tangled.

The nurse bustles out of the room after telling me to stay put. She returns quickly, frowning when she sees me swaying where I sit. "He can stay."

Landon guides me back down on the bed, with a grateful thanks to the nurse, and folds me back into his arms. She gives a gentle, but tired smile as I fade out as quickly as I came to.

chapter
twenty-six

Allie

Since I'm too sore to sleep on an air mattress and go hiking, Landon cancels our vacation with the promise that we'll go once I'm feeling better. Instead, I shift my time off to sick time and he packs up PeeWee to come stay with me and Blade.

For the first week, I absolutely love having him dote on me. My body aches in ways I've never felt, and having Landon with me makes me feel safe. By the end of the first week, I'm going stir-crazy from being housebound and not having any space to myself. I love Landon, but he's in overprotective mode and it's becoming a little much.

"I think I'm going to go out, do a little shopping." My voice is determined, ready to win the argument I know is coming. I'm already dressed and ready to go, less time for him to argue with me.

"I guess we have been pretty cooped up in the house." He smiles and rests his hand on my arm and kisses my cheek. "Give me ten minutes and we can head out."

"Landon, I appreciate how helpful you've been this past week, but I was hoping to have some alone time." Biting my lip, I fight the crushing guilt at the hurt look on his face. He's trying so hard to be there for me, to ensure I have everything I need, and it feels like I'm throwing it in his face.

When he sighs and smiles, I wrap my arms around him more grateful than I can express over how wonderful he is. "I just want to help. Go, have fun. I'll see you when you get home. Maybe I'll take PeeWee for a walk."

Heading out, I decide to go to the mall and just wander through my favorite stores. As I drive, I find myself looking at my town with new eyes. Every person on the street looks suspicious and I find myself wondering which of the men I see is the one who tried to violate me in the worst way.

My safe home has been painted with a new brush and I don't like it. I want the rose-colored glasses back. I don't want to think twice about going for a walk after dark. I don't want to feel like I need to check over my shoulder when I'm out.

Lost in my thoughts, I drive mindlessly through town and into the parking lot. Shutting my car off, I step out and finally process my surroundings. I'm at work.

Breathing hard, I start to open my car door again, but instead I drop my hand and with unsteady footsteps, I slowly make my way into the center of the park. My heart pounds, my chest feels constricted as I take slow steps.

I've lost my damn mind, but I can't seem to pull myself away. Maybe it's just morbid curiosity, but I need to look at the place where just a week ago I was pinned down. I need to face the space that I designed to be a Zen garden, but is now I place that has been haunting my nightmares.

Tears fill my eyes as I kick my flip flops off and step onto the stones at the base of the fountain, just like that day. This time, however, I'm more watchful of my surroundings.

Taking a deep breath, I turn to face the bench I was thrown down on. It looks exactly the same as it did before. Of course it does. If our environment changed to reflect the horrific things that happened in it, the world would be an ugly place. Instead, most of humanity's ugliness is disguised, with a few exceptions of course.

The air flowing in and out of my lungs is choking me as I try to prevent the feeling of suffocation and panic. I can't seem to fill my lungs enough.

Biting my fist, I stifle back a sob as my knees buckle and I collapse to the ground. Planting my hands on the smooth stones, I let myself release the tears, the flowing water washing them away. I'm completely shaken, and I don't know how to find some sort of peace again.

My head jerks up, a scream flying from my lips when a hand lands on my shoulders. My vision is blurry as I pummel the person touching me with my fists.

"Shhh. Allie, it's me. It's Landon." His face fills my blurred vision before I collapse weakly into his arms. His soft, soothing whispers calming me while my body stops convulsing with the power of my sobs.

I don't know how much time passes before the tears stops and my breathing evens out. Stepping back, I rub my hands over my arms trying to warm up.

"Why are you here, Landon?" My voice is quiet, resigned. The hoarseness scratching my throat. My entire body hurts.

"I followed you. I know you, Allie. I knew you would end up here." When he steps toward me, I take a quick step back.

"I told you I wanted to be alone, just for an afternoon. I'm a grown woman, I'm capable of dealing with this. I just wanted you to leave me alone." I know my words hurt him. I know he's trying to help. That doesn't change the fact that I need time to myself to deal with what happened. I like to believe I will be able to move past it, but I need to confront as much of it as I can. And I want to do that on my own.

"Allie, I can't just leave you alone." He sounds tired, and for the first time I notice the dark circles under his eyes. How could I have missed them?

"Yes, you can. I love having you stay with me, but you don't need to sacrifice your time to yourself just because this happened." My words are harsh, completely unfair, but I can't seem to find my filter.

"You're wrong. It's not a sacrifice. And yes, I do need to be with you. I need to make sure you're okay." His quiet, steady demeanor just fuels my irrational anger.

"Why? Why are you putting this on yourself?" I raise my voice. I hate feeling dependent on anyone and right now it feels like he is bearing the weight of our relationship. I want him to have an equal partner in me, I don't want him to feel like I'm a burden.

"Because it's my fault!" he yells, dropping his voice when I flinch. "You were attacked because of me. You were attacked because I was late. That's why. That's why I need to make sure you're okay. If you're okay, then we'll be okay. I need you to know I won't let you down again. I can't sleep because all I can think about is losing you. Losing you because one day you'll wake up and resent me for letting this happen to you."

He looks so tormented, it breaks my heart and suddenly I see the whole situation from his point of view. I finally recognize what I'm seeing in his eyes, a desperate need to make things right. Rushing forward, I wrap my arms around him.

"It's not your fault. It's not. There's only one person to blame, and that's the sick person who attacked me. He's the only one at fault. If it wasn't me, it would've been someone else. I could've stayed inside, but I didn't. That doesn't make it my fault. We can't take that on because it just releases him from his guilt." As I speak the words, I feel a piece of me click back together.

I'm nowhere near healed, this will be an emotional scar that will last a lifetime, but vocalizing that it was a conscious decision of a person who saw an opportunity helps me realize I was holding some of the blame. I don't want that for either of us.

Landon presses his forehead to mine, our eyes locked on each other. In this moment we're holding each other together, stabilizing, and I know that no matter what comes our way, I will fight for us always to be the other's safe place. That's what love is about. It's not about equal playing fields. It's about creating a balance that works for us and knowing it's okay for it to tip one way or the other, because eventually it will even out again.

"I love you, Allie. Maybe here, in this place, isn't the best spot to tell you, but I need you to hear the words. I need you to know that I won't leave you alone when you're hurting, because that's what you do for someone you love." He searches my eyes, his hands kneading gentle circles in my lower back.

"I love you too." My voice is quiet, sure. It's the one thing I'm one hundred percent certain of.

He kisses me, deep and passionately. Every feeling we've been holding onto, fear, anger, guilt, love; it's all poured into this kiss. And it's perfect.

Landon has colored this place with a positive memory. It'll always hold a shadow, it may not be the place it once was, but this moment will always be bigger.

"Thank you for returning some of the peace to my Zen garden." Burying my face into his chest, I breathe in deeply. "Let's go home."

chapter twenty-seven

Landon

Once we get home, Allie goes to take a warm bath and I set about prepping dinner. I knew she would go to that garden, I could feel it. I'm so glad I followed that feeling and showed up. A weight has been lifted, telling her how I feel like it's my fault, and her conviction when she took both of us out of the equation and reminded me it's no one's fault but that *guy's*.

Now that some of her physical aches have eased, her ribs the biggest source of contention, she's returning to work next week. I can see the conflicting emotions she's struggling with when she talks about going back there, but maybe today will help.

By the time Allie gets out of the tub, dinner is on the table.

"This looks so good!" Allie gushes.

It's a simple casserole, but I made sure to add in extra pepper jack cheese, her favorite.

"While I was cooking, I was thinking you should call Dawn and Blake up. You've been avoiding Dawn since the hospital. Plus Blake sounded really upset when you were talking to her last night." My voice is gentle, but she needs to talk to them, to someone, about what happened.

"You're right. I know Dawn will want to talk more about the Brendan thing, even though it's unnecessary. Blake returned yesterday from her vacation, I know speaking on the phone last night wasn't enough to appease her, she was mad no one told her about what happened. I said I didn't want to ruin her vacation." Allie sets her fork down, the wince when she reaches for the pitcher of iced tea barely discernible, but I don't miss it. I know better than to say anything, we've argued enough over me trying to do too much for her.

PeeWee barks at Blade, who is perched on his cat tower. Grinning, I glance over at Allie. "I think he likes living here with his buddy."

Allie's fork pauses mid-air as she looks over to where PeeWee is wiggling his butt, waiting for Blade to play. "They definitely get along." She clears her throat, glancing back at me. "Landon, I love having you here, but I think maybe you should go home. I know how hard it is for you not to do things for me, but I need to get back into my own routine. It's not that I don't love having you here, but—"

"But you're ready to have your space back. I understand. It's going to be impossible not to worry, but I'll head home tomorrow, if that's okay." I smile at her, trying to hide how disappointed I am. I don't want to go back home. Living with Allie has been a dream come true, but I know she's not ready for that.

"Thank you for understanding. I was thinking, maybe you should keep your key." She watches me, her lips quirking as I visibly try to contain my excitement.

"Really?" She nods.

It's still so surreal, we're here and we're actually moving forward. She's starting to trust that I'm not going anywhere this time, and I'm going to continue to show her how much I love her and that I will do anything to make her happy.

"I love you. I'll make you a key this week. I just need to let Josh know so he quits walking around in his underwear." We grin at each other.

Allie made the mistake of walking in the house the other day when I went to grab some more clothes and got a glimpse of Josh pulling his boxers up over his ass. He really has no shame.

"Yeah, that was scarring. We should introduce him to Blake." Laughing, she shakes her head. "She would eat him up and spit him out."

Allie's not lying, but as much as I love my brother, I would love to see it. Though, we both know that Josh isn't Blake's type.

At the end of the night, we curl up in her bed. I listen to her steady breathing, grateful that she's sleeping peacefully. The first few nights she had such bad nightmares, she punched me in the face.

Kissing her shoulder, I close my eyes and fall asleep grateful that it's next to Allie. Every night, I say thanks for my second chance.

chapter
twenty-eight

Allie

Tonight is my first night in my condo without Landon since the attack. Instead of facing the emptiness, I invited Dawn and Blake over for pizza and a movie. It's kind of sad, but I also want to catch up with them now that things have settled a little more, and without Landon hovering like a neurotic hen in the background.

"Come in," I holler when I hear a knock on the door, I look up from where I'm laying out snacks on the coffee table to grin at Blake.

"You're early." I snag a carrot and dunk it into my homemade dill dip. God, that's so good.

"Yeah, I wanted to talk to you about something before Dawn got here." Blake's tone is uncharacteristically serious, so I sit down.

"What is it?" I'm curious, this is different than the hysterics she was in when we spoke on the phone and I told her what happened.

"I want you to know, I'm on your side with the whole Dawn and Brendan thing. She should've come to you before anything happened. I told her that." Blake is serious, her eyes unhappy as she paces my living room. "I can't believe she acted on it, and with everything that's been going on."

I hate that her concern for me is causing a rift between her and her twin, especially when she's carrying a burden she doesn't need to.

Sighing, I pat the couch next to me. "Blake, I've known for a long time that Dawn is attracted to Brendan. I'm glad they're happy." My voice is sincere because I truly mean the words.

Before Blake can reply, Dawn pokes her head in. "Hey."

She comes in, hugging me as she sets a bottle of wine down on the table. Her and Blake are giving each other the side eye as she sits in the chair on my other side. This needs to end.

"Okay you two. Enough." I stand up and cross my arms, ignoring the pain in my ribs. "Listen up, you need to stop arguing over this. I'm glad that you and Brendan are happy. I really don't care that you didn't talk to me about it, maybe before everything happened I would have, but not anymore."

They finally start to relax, I know they will need to work this out between themselves later.

A knock on the door makes me tense, my eyes watchful as Blake gets up and opens the door. Only relaxing when I see the pizza in the guy's hands, I turn back to my drink. Dawn's eyes are watchful as Blake pays and brings the box of cheesy goodness to the table.

"How're you doing?" Dawn's voice is soft.

My heart starts pounding in my chest, I hate talking about it, but I know I need to get it out. I spared Landon many of the details, I just couldn't bear to put that burden on him, but I know it's different with Blake and Dawn.

"Everything's different. I still feel him pressed against me, the cruelty in his intent. I'm forever grateful to whomever came to my rescue, and the worst part is I can't even say thank you because they don't want to be known. This town is different to me, my work is—just not the same anymore. It used to be a place I enjoyed, a place I actually looked forward to going to every day. That feeling is gone. There are days when I don't even know how I'm going to leave the house." My voice shakes. "Landon has been so great. I'm worried that he's not going to want to deal with the repercussions of this. I haven't been able to bring myself to have sex with him since then. He thinks it's because of my ribs, but, in reality, sex is tainted. I feel like my body was stolen from me, even though nothing happened. Well, not nothing, you know what I mean."

They listen as I cry through the myriad of feelings I get ambushed with every day. I can't even imagine how someone who was raped deals with the emotions and the anger and the fear on a day to day basis.

"Allie, hardly any time has passed. No one expects you to just get over it. And if they do, they're not worth your time." Blake stands up, her voice defensive.

I know this, I really do, but I wish I could get over it. I just want to feel normal again.

"Things with Landon will come. You love each other. Talk to him, ease back into it at your own pace. Remember what he said to you, not to let anyone steal your joy. Don't give that sicko that kind of power over your body." Dawn comes over and takes my hand, her eyes wet with unshed tears.

Blake sits on my other side, taking my other hand, and for a little while we just sit there. I can feel their comfort flowing into me. I left the garden with so much resolve, but it's amazing how quickly that dissipated.

"You're right. I know none of this is my fault. And I don't want him to have any power over me." I squeeze their hands before letting go so we can eat.

My mind is going a mile a minute as I think about the best way to deal with this before I finally remember the card I was given when I was discharged from the hospital. The therapist specializes in victims of sexual assault, and I think that even just a few sessions will help me.

Maybe some people are strong enough to deal on their own, but I think having a professional to talk to will help me.

We eat in silence, lost in the dark place that comes when something horrible happens to you or someone you know. They both sense I need to shift gears, but I can tell they aren't sure where to go from here.

Finishing off my slice of pizza, I sink into the couch getting cozy and angle my body toward Dawn. "Now, why don't you tell me how the whole you and Brendan thing got started, I want to hear the dirt. Well, maybe not the naughty bits because awkward." I grin at Dawn. I want to hear, but I also want to avoid talking about me right now. I still haven't sorted out how to cope with everything.

"I went to his house for his birthday, brought him a tuxedo cupcake. We ended up sharing it and then he kissed me." She blushes, chewing on her lower lip. "I've liked Brendan for a long time, and I loved kissing him, but I told him I wouldn't be his rebound and left."

She smirks, blushing a little more before she continues, "So we kept talking, but never broached the topic of the kiss again, so I let it go. Then one day he shows up at my door and says I'm not a rebound and asked to come in. I told him all I want is a fair chance and he promised me that's what we would do, give 'us' a fair chance."

She's so happy, she's glowing by the time she's filled us in on everything that's been happening since March.

"I'm so happy for you two. Seriously, I think you're such a good match and I truly hope it works. I think I said the same thing to Landon not long after we started. All anyone really wants is a fair chance to get their happily ever after." I smile, feeling my lips wobble a little with emotion. Leaning forward, I snag another piece of pizza to give me a chance to compose myself. I've been feeling so emotional lately.

"Yeah yeah. You're happy, she's happy. Now, let's get on to the important shit. Girls' trip. Florida. A sandy beach and my two best friends. It's happening this year. I don't want to go hiking. I don't want to go to Vegas. I want to go to the beach. And *Harry Potter World*. No more putting it off." Blake points at us, her gaze no-nonsense.

Laughing we start planning our annual girls' trip. It's a nice reprieve to focus on something other than what happened. By the time they leave, I feel okay to crawl into my bed alone, something I wasn't sure I would be after Landon took his stuff and went home for the night.

chapter
twenty-nine

August

Landon

A fire crackles in the pit, the scent of burning pine filling our campsite. Allie loads the table with everything we need to cook dinner over the fire. Smiling as she hums, I get the grill ready while watching her. All the physical signs of her attack have vanished, her ribs healed and the bruises gone.

It's been a couple of months since that night and we're finally on our vacation. Allie wanted to take the time to not only heal physically, but address some of the mental issues that followed before we did this.

"Tomorrow we should rent a canoe and circle the lake that way. If it's hot enough, maybe we can brave the cool water and go swimming. I also want to explore the island in the middle of the lake." Allie drops into her chair, a fresh beer in hand.

Taking the bottle she offers me, I scooch closer to her and drape one arm across her shoulders. "Sounds fun."

"Wait, you're not going to argue with me?" She gives me some serious side eye.

After our moment in the garden outside her office, I tried not to be as overprotective. I didn't always succeed, and we had several arguments about expectations in our relationship after Allie asked me to let her be on her own. As much as I hated not being there all the time, I can admit she was right. I was constantly in her space trying to stop her from doing things because I was paranoid she would hurt herself. And I couldn't see her doing those things and it helped me worry a little less. A very little less, but it did help.

"Is there any point?" I give an exaggerated sigh, winking at her. "Besides, I can admit I was being a little overbearing and ridiculous."

She laughs, leaning forward to flip the steak I have cooking on the grill.

It's nice to see her laughing more. Allie is strong, and she tried not to let the attack change her, but something like that impacts the way our brain processes things. She doesn't look at things the same and it's been an adjustment for the both of us to constantly confront how she's changed.

Allie is still strong, she loves to laugh and smile, but her view of the world isn't quite as positive as it was before. She's more cautious about her approach to the outside world.

I wish for her that she didn't need to feel so guarded, but I don't know how she could possibly come back from what happened without any changes.

She's a little more somber, a little less trusting than she was before.

Yet, she also recognizes that the good will always outweigh the bad and she's unwilling to let some asshole steal her light.

We still argue about things, like me wanting to move in with her and her telling me it's too soon. Or when she didn't tell me that she slipped in the shower the day after I returned home and torqued her ribs.

It's been an interesting journey as we navigate our relationship in a way we never had a chance to before. I love every moment of it, and if I thought she would say yes, I would ask her to marry me right now. But Allie doesn't want to rush. She wants to take things slow and "do it right" in her words.

Our views on where our relationship is at are completely different, but I can wait. My heart held on to her for over seven years, it can wait a couple more before we take the next step. She's the love of my life and we have the rest of our lives to reach those milestones.

epilogue

One Year Later

"Now let's raise our glasses. To Dawn and Brendan, congrats on your beautiful wedding. We can't wait to see what the future holds for you and that darling baby boy." Everyone tilts their glasses back, sipping at the champagne as Dawn and Brendan kiss. Kyler chews on his fist next to them, his chin covered in saliva as he smiles around his hand.

Sitting next to Landon, I kiss him on the cheek.

"They look so happy," he observes.

And they do. Dawn is glowing, despite the exhaustion that goes hand in hand with having a three-month-old infant. Brendan has never looked happier or more in love. He smiles at me, lifting his glass at Landon and me before turning to whisper in Dawn's ear.

I'm so glad they've found their happiness. It was a bit of a shock for all of us when Dawn announced over brunch that not only were she and Brendan moving in together, but that they were expecting a child and getting married.

It took me a while to process that, not because I was jealous, but because it made me realize that when something is right it doesn't matter about a timeline.

Four weeks later, Landon moved in with me.

And tonight, I get to tell him that he's going to be a father. The sparkling apple juice in my glass disguising the fact that I'm not drinking. Blake has been helping me hide the fact I'm pregnant from everyone. I needed an ally at the wedding and I have something special planned for Landon later, so I confided in Blake because I knew she would help keep my secret.

Leaning into Landon, I sigh.

"What's going on in that beautiful head of yours?" He kisses me on my temple, smiling as I tilt my head back to look at him.

"I'm just happy." I resist rubbing my hand over my stomach, taking his hand instead.

We've overcome so much in the last year. The counseling helped me enormously, I feel capable of managing the rare moments of fear, something that seemed impossible as I started needing to cope with the outside world a little more.

Another woman was assaulted, but this time someone saw who the perpetrator was and he's currently being charged. I don't know if the guy is the same person who attacked me, but I tell myself he is and that he's finally getting what he deserves.

"Let's dance." Landon stands, pulling me with him as he backs onto the dance floor.

I rest my cheek on his chest as we sway back and forth

in time to the music.

Two years ago I never would have thought I would be dancing with Landon at Brendan's wedding to one of my best friends. Life has a funny way of working out when you trust yourself and follow your heart. My heart knew Landon was meant for me, just like Dawn knew her heart was meant for Brendan. We just had to wait for the timing to be right.

The question was never why not me. I should have been asking myself why not now. Our time is here and I've never been happier.

about
ashley erin

Ashley Erin lives in Alberta, Canada where winter and summer compete to take over. She wars flip flops as soon as it's above freezing, because her hatred of socks outweighs her dislike of snow. Her boyfriend stays with her despite a penchant for adopting rescued cats and dogs without permission. Their two dogs and four cats are spoiled rotten. When Ashley isn't writing, she is reading or working with horses.

Ashley is a self-published author of contemporary and new adult romance.

www.ingramcontent.com/pod-product-compliance
Lightning Source LLC
Chambersburg PA
CBHW021012120726
47905CB00009B/2981